AMONG US

A Traitor
in Space

Published in French under the title *Among us : Un traître dans l'espace*

© 2021 404 éditions, a division of Édi8, Paris, France

Among Us is a registered trademark of Innersloth LLC. All rights reserved.

This book is not an official *Among Us* product. It is not approved by or related
to Innersloth LLC.

Andrews McMeel Publishing
a division of Andrews McMeel Universal
1130 Walnut Street, Kansas City, Missouri 64106
www.andrewsmcmeel.com

21 22 23 24 25 RR2 10 9 8 7 6 5 4 3 2 1

ISBN: 978-1-5248-7154-3

Library of Congress Control Number: 2021943025

Made by:
Lakeside Book Company
Address and location of manufacturer:
1009 Sloan Street
Crawfordsville, IN 47933
1st Printing – 8/30/21

ATTENTION: SCHOOLS AND BUSINESSES
Andrews McMeel books are available at quantity discounts with bulk
purchase for educational, business, or sales promotional use. For information,
please e-mail the Andrews McMeel Publishing Special Sales Department:
specialsales@amuniversal.com.

AMONG US

A Traitor in Space

LAURA RIVIÈRE

Illustrated by Théo Berthet

WITHDRAWN

AN UNOFFICIAL ADVENTURE

Andrews McMeel
PUBLISHING®

Chapter 1

Apparently I'm lost again. I open the map of the *Skeld*, which instantly appears on the inside of my helmet visor. This ship is such a maze! And a damn crazy one at that. The confusing layout isn't to MIRA's usual standards at all. It's like they found an old ship from who knows where and slapped on just enough updates to operate it. Seriously, the whole thing is poorly planned. Like, the beds are located in sleeping pods along the hallway between the Cafeteria and Upper Engine. Who does this? It's as if the person who designed this forgot to include rooms and just added pods wherever there was space. Who wants to sleep near engine noise and Cafeteria smells? Even the beds in MedBay seem more comfortable than the capsules we lock ourselves in for eight hours every day. I'll just get used to it, I guess.

Until then, I'm on another useless detour. I was supposed to be going to Storage, and somehow I've ended up in Navigation. Which is weirdly empty. I thought Janelle was supposed to be working here this afternoon.

I leave Navigation and almost walk right into her. The bright pink of her spacesuit takes me by surprise as always, and I can't help but step back. She jumps a bit too.

"Valdemar! You scared me!" she exclaims. "What are you doing here? I thought you were in Storage."

"Me too," I say.

"Huh? What do you mean?"

"I thought I was in Storage too, but I got lost again!"

I can tell Janelle doesn't appreciate my attempt at a joke, but she still forces out a polite laugh.

"V, it's been three weeks. It's about time you actually figured this all out. That can't always be your excuse." She winks and moves aside so I can get by.

I take a right. If the map is accurate, it will be faster than turning around. After only a few yards, I hear Janelle's voice echo behind me again.

"Uh, V, where are you going?" she asks nervously.

"I'm going to go through the Cafeteria. It's easier to get to Stor—"

"The Cafeteria? No . . . um, I have to go, um, check something in Communications. Should we just go together?"

What's wrong with her? I've never seen her act so strange. If I didn't know that she was into women and already with someone, I'd swear she was flirting with me. She keeps avoiding my eyes as she's talking.

I reluctantly go along with her suggestion. I've already wasted too much time, but I'm curious.

"What are you up to in Communications?" I ask her on the way.

"I have data to upload," she answers a little too quickly.

"Again? But weren't you there already this morning?"

"Yes! But I'm not done. I was, um, interrupted."

This doesn't make any sense.

"By Livia!" she adds, almost shouting.

Oh! That's all I need to know. Whatever those two lovebirds were up to, I hope they were careful to not get caught on camera.

We split up when we get to Communications. Janelle enters and settles in front of the monitor. From the outside, it's impossible to see if she really is downloading something. When she turns around to see where I am, I hurry on my way so she doesn't think I've been watching her. I'd prefer to wait there though. I still get the feeling she lied to me, like she'll leave as soon as I go around the corner. But I'm already so far behind in my tasks for today, so I drop it. Maybe I'll figure out what's going on later.

When I get to Storage, I see Flavius just standing there, swinging his arms in the middle of the room. His yellow spacesuit is surprisingly clean for once. And he's got his usual pink plastic flower on his head. When he notices me, he jumps.

Really? Am I that scary?

I wonder what he's doing. Especially since . . . he's not doing anything! This is the third time I've seen him just hanging about. Sure, he's new. He just completed his training at MIRA HQ, and this is his first active ship assignment. Even so, he's been acting really strange.

"Have you finished your tasks?" I ask.

"Yeah. Well, almost. I've still got some to do . . . in Admin. I'm . . . I'm gonna go now. See you later, Valdemar!"

"Please just call me 'V' like everyone else."

"Um, okay. See you, V!"

And just like that, he saunters away without having touched anything in the room.

Seriously, why is everyone so weird today? First Janelle, now Flavius. What's wrong with them? I'll have to talk with Doc about it tonight after work—she's the biggest gossip on the ship.

Until then, I try to collect myself by focusing on my work. I've almost completed my tasks for the day. I saved Storage for last because it's one of the things I hate the most. It's such a pain. I have to refuel the engines, and the fuel can, as usual, hasn't been cleaned.

Even through my spacesuit, I can tell how sticky it is. And it's slippery too. Our spacesuits are good, practical for most things, but the gloves could be better. They don't work at all with some tasks—like this one. If you've got big hands like I do, it's impossible to fit through this handle!

You have to grab it the best you can with both hands and be careful to not drop it, carrying it around awkwardly to one of the two engines. The lower one, in this case. But even when you've managed to do all that, it gets harder: you have to hold it in just the right way to pour the contents into the tank without getting it all over your hands. It's hell.

Well, here goes nothing. I grab the can, struggling to find a stable grip.

I approach the fuel tank and . . . of course, I forgot to open it.

I gently put the can down, place my glove on the scanner, and the small hatch opens.

I grab my fuel can, lift it up, and keep tilting it more and more as it empties into the tank. I've got to stay like this for a few minutes while the tank gauge reaches the recommended level. I'm sighing so hard I bet they can hear me all the way on the other side of the ship.

I'm almost halfway through when a sudden, shrill noise makes me flinch. I drop the can to the ground, hurling fuel everywhere.

"Shi—"

What the hell is going on? The noise keeps blaring. And now there's a flashing light too.

Oh, I remember: it's the alarm for emergency meetings! That's no joke. I'll have to leave my task unfinished and start all over later.

I've done a few missions before, and emergency meetings (as the name suggests) are kind of unusual. So, of course, I panic.

What's going on? Are we crashing? I'm too young to die! I'm not even twenty yet!

My heart is pounding. Too bad about the fuel—I'll just have to clean up later. I head straight for the Cafeteria. That's where the primary emergency panel is, and it's the designated meeting area in case of an alarm.

This is a first for me. And I don't think I'm going to like it.

I don't see anyone on the way to the Cafeteria, which is odd. Are they all already there? I break into a sprint. When I get there, the door is closed. I stop for a few seconds, enough time to catch my breath and calm down a little. What's going to be behind this door?

Then I notice that I'm not even at the Cafeteria at all. In my panic, I went the wrong way again and ended up in Communications. Janelle is gone. I still don't believe her. . . . She probably left just after me.

I'm sweating profusely in my purple spacesuit. I have to hurry if I want to make it out of this alive.

With a tap to the controls on my helmet, I summon the map to my visor again. Only my gloves are covered in grease and my fingers slip across the screen, leaving fuel all over the place. And all my files open on the screen—except the one I need, of course. When I finally manage to open the map, I let out a huge sigh of relief. But the relief is short-lived: I know where I need to go now, but my visor is so dirty that I can't even see a foot ahead of me! How am I supposed to find my way to the Cafeteria?

Just as I'm about to lift my visor to see clearly, I stop. What if someone set off the alarm because the ship is low on oxygen? Or worse, what if there's some toxic gas in the ship? That would be a stupid way to go. It's one of the

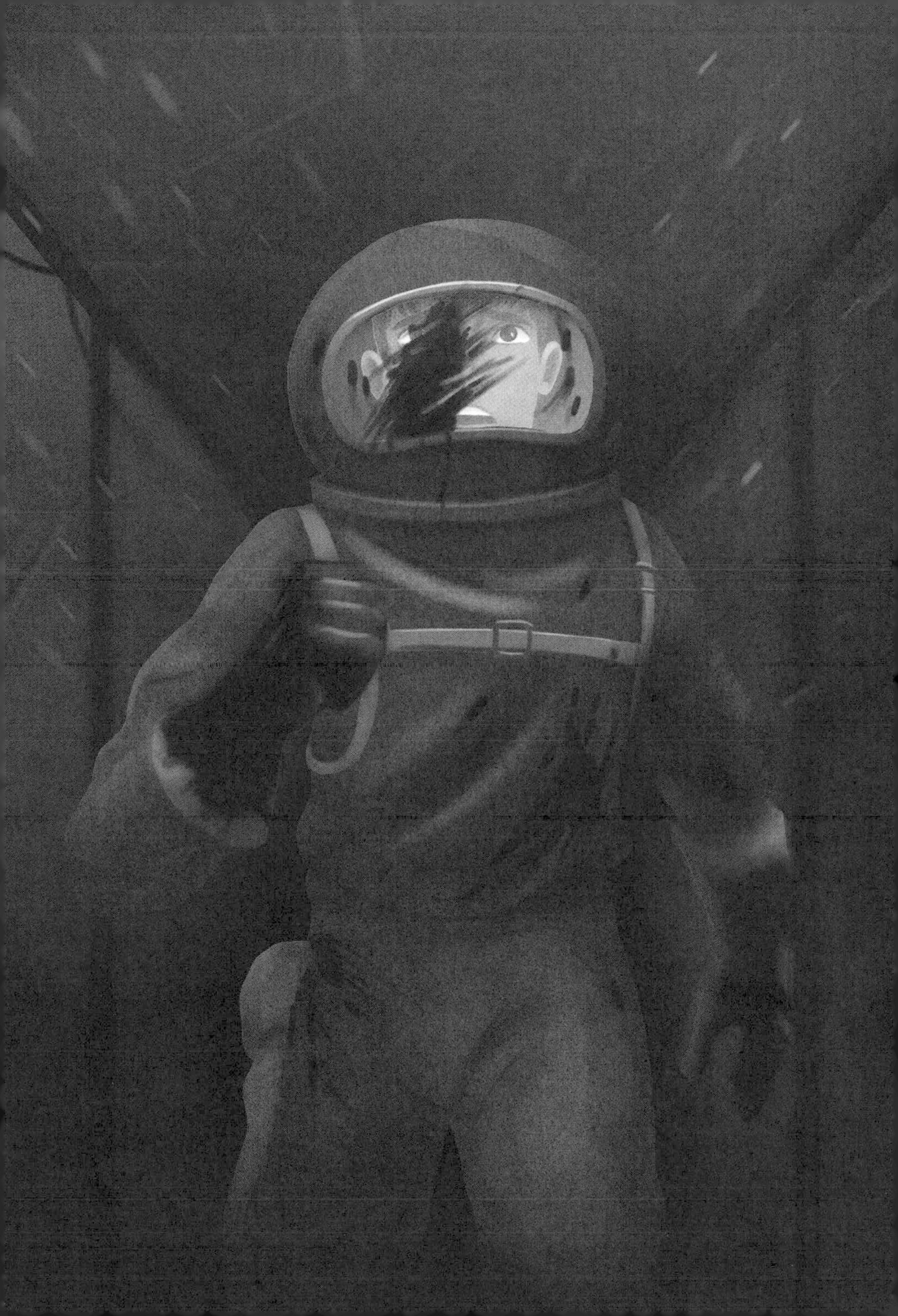

first things every kid learns: if there's any kind of danger or alarm, don't lift your visor, remove your helmet, or leave your oxygen behind. The basics.

My heart is beating way too fast. It feels like it's about the burst out of my chest. Trembling, I grope the walls and make my way left. Once I get to Storage, I just have to go right. Easy enough! But I still need to hurry. Despite the fact that I can't see, I decide to start running. Brilliant idea. I barely make it into Storage before my knee gets in a fight with a big metal crate and loses, sending me face-first into the ground. If I make it out of this alive, I'll have to remind myself to do something about that. This room needs some cleaning.

I struggle to get up. The noise from the alarm is intense. And the flashing light, distorted by the grease on my helmet, is overwhelming. Please make this stop. And let me make it out of this alive!

I somehow manage to reach the hallway that leads to the Cafeteria. Finally, there's nothing in my way. I sprint down the hall—after all, my life may depend on it. Surely, there are others near. I scream at the top of my lungs, "Where are you?! Hello? Is anyone there?"

My voice is the only one I hear. Since the alarm went off, I haven't seen anyone. Where could they be? Shouldn't I have heard them by now? Is there some protocol I've forgotten? Am I going to die here, all alone, covered in muck?

I mentally prepare for my last moments. . . . Whatever happens now, I must above all be dignified.

When I make it to the Cafeteria, almost everyone is already there: Doc, the Stark-Liu family, Flavius, JC, Janelle, and Livia. All eyes are on me. And they look serious.

What happened?

Chapter 2

I don't have time to ask them anything before the lights in the Cafeteria go out. My heart is thundering. What is going on? Here I was thinking I was finally safe! It's like my life is flashing before my eyes. Well, mostly just regrets. This really isn't how I'd pictured the end.

There's movement around me. I hear footsteps, things being shifted.

Suddenly, JC, our self-proclaimed leader, breaks the silence. "V, go get the power back up and running. Quickly!"

Running. Ha, ha. He thinks he's funny.

It takes me a little while to react. And when I finally get going, I bump into everything, including the wall. Damn ship!

JC is laughing. "Come on, V, you're no rookie. You've got to know how a circuit breaker works."

Obviously. I also know what it looks like. But here, in the dark, in a second-rate ship I'm still getting lost in, things are a bit more complicated. I try to keep calm. I know that JC is just waiting for me to lose it.

I take a deep breath and focus on my task.

"On your left, I think." The whisper is not even that quiet. It's Doc, always ready to give me a hand.

I follow her suggestion and find the switch. Finally! It's a bit stiff, but I put some muscle into it and manage to flip it. With a loud CLICK, the power is restored, *and there was light.* I feel a smile spread across my face. I'm pretty proud of myself.

When I turn around, I notice that every crewmate is standing around the table, looking at me. Through my grease-smeared visor, I can see that a bunch of them are wearing silly hats. There are a bunch of colorful balloons behind JC's back, and the table is covered with all kinds of food. Huh?

"Happy birthday, V!" they yell in unison.

I'm half grateful, half deeply annoyed. On one hand, I am glad that my crewmates remembered my birthday and went as far as preparing this little surprise for me. On the other, I want to strangle them all and yell, *"ALL THAT FOR THIS?!"* But that might get me into trouble, so I play nice.

"Wow . . . um . . . thank you. I didn't expect this at all!"

The truth is, I really do feel embarrassed. Seriously, if they knew what had been going through my mind . . . I was convinced that aliens had taken control of the ship, or that one of us had gone rogue and was going after everyone else with an ax! Luckily, my wild imaginings will remain just that: imagined.

"See? I told you so. He doesn't look all that happy," says JC.

"No! It's . . . it's really nice," I protest. "Really!"

"Really?" Flavius asks. "You don't look like you think it is."

"It is! It's just . . . um . . ."

"That we scared the crap out of you, right? Admit it!" Janelle says.

"Not at all!" I reply, way too fast to be believable.

"Come on! You can tell us, V. I saw that you weren't yourself when we met in Navigation."

"You did look really suspicious when you saw me in Storage," adds Flavius.

"Come on! Is this my birthday or a trial?"

Here I go again. Someone messes with me, and it sets me off. It's got to be one of my biggest flaws. I'm working on it, but it's easier said than done.

"We should eat the cake before the icing runs completely off it," Doc says.

At least she has my back. It makes you wonder how I got through life during all those years when we'd lost touch. I'd really missed having someone around I could rely on like this.

Janelle starts cutting slices of the huge cake (we'll be eating it for days, I'm sure) while our oldest crewmate, Henry, who wears a spacesuit so white it's hard to look at, serves them.

My heart rate finally returns to normal. I sure hope I don't have to deal with this kind of situation too often. I don't know if I could manage. Clearly I'm too high-strung for surprises. I avoid them as much as possible, which is why I chose to crew on patrol vessels. The job is quiet and, above all, very routine. I live my life and do my tasks. It's that simple. But community life inevitably has its share of the unexpected, so you have to live with it. I imagine it'd be hard to avoid it unless you live on your own, like some hermit. And I don't think I could do that either. Life is about compromise, right?

"Shorry. It was my idea." Doc sits next to me, mouth full, visor up.

I realize mine is still dirty and down. Damn alarm!

"Hmm?" I reply.

"The surprise. Sorry, it's my fault; I thought you would like it," she continues.

"Oh, that's fine. It's nice, really. It's just . . ." I exhale. "It's just that I'm not used to this anymore."

"Oh? You haven't celebrated since . . . ?"

I nod.

"I'm sorry. Really. I hope it didn't bring all that back. . . ."

"Don't worry, Doc, I'm fine. Actually, I think it feels good to enjoy these simple things. And even back then, we didn't really celebrate. Most of the time, they weren't even there."

Doc puts her spoon down on her plate and her arm around my shoulder. I smile so I don't cry. I could shed a few tears and no one would see a thing through my dirty visor, but I try to retain some dignity.

Doc tightens her embrace just a bit. I think she feels guilty for not having been there during those difficult years. But she couldn't have known.

I remember the expression on her face a few days after our big reunion on this ship when I told her. She'd been so excited to tell me all about what was going on with her parents and how proud she was of her successes in biomedicine.

Then she asked, "What about you?" and something broke inside me. I told her that after my fathers died during a mission, I had been handed off from uncle to aunt to distant friends. I just spat out the news without any preamble to soften the blow. Even after all these years, I'm still never quite sure how to talk about it. "Hello. I have been an orphan since I was twelve years old" isn't the best introduction. But I'm not a fan of withholding information or avoiding reality.

I saw the shock on Doc's face even through her visor. She was suddenly speechless. The last time she'd seen me, I was her cheerful eleven-year-old neighbor who followed her everywhere. I was like her little brother. She'd known my fathers well. That is, as much as anyone could get to know them, given they were always away on long missions. But she quickly recovered from her shock. And in no time, we became good friends once again, as though nothing had happened, as though we had never parted, as though it hadn't been eight years.

As I hug Doc in the Cafeteria, the mood suddenly feels heavy, and I have to find something to lighten it.

"So, you thought that sabotaging the ship and activating the emergency alarm was a good idea for a birthday surprise?"

Doc releases her grip before answering me. "Not really. I just wanted to surprise you. I asked everyone for help and found some great coconspirators."

"Flavius and Janelle?"

"Among others, yes. Everyone was up for it, actually. But Janelle really took the project to another level."

"I can't believe JC let you do that."

"You know JC's not *really* our boss, right? He's just got more experience, that's all. Our contracts have us all on equal footing here. And we decided democratically. The overwhelming majority agreed to organize a surprise birthday party for our very own V."

I shrug. Although I understand why Doc did all of this for me, I don't get why the others got so involved. I mean, most of us have only known each other for three short weeks. In the other ships I've worked on, this kind of group activity wasn't really common.

"Oh, you know," Doc says. "I think we all needed a little break from the routine. A little disruption every now and then doesn't hurt, right?"

I didn't remember Doc as a particularly reckless and adventurous person. She was nitpicky, bossy, and a bit of a know-it-all. That's how she got her nickname. One time, she'd disagreed with a teacher on some incidental point, so she ran experiment after experiment just to prove to him that *she* was right. She hadn't even been eleven. Everyone at school then started calling her "Doc" because of the tone she'd taken (and that she often takes, even now) when stating her opinions. I started calling her that, too, after she recounted the story with more than a hint of pride.

As the conversation begins to wind down among the cake-stuffed crew, a funny bell rings throughout the Cafeteria.

"Recess is over!" JC yells. "Let's pack it up!"

Doc gets up and begins to clear the table.

"Huh. I thought he wasn't our boss," I whisper.

"No, but we all agreed. Two hours, and then we all get back to work. We still have a ship to run, you know? Unless you've suddenly started enjoying parties."

There's the Doc I know again: rules are rules.

Chapter 3

The next morning, I wake up early, but I hang out in bed longer than usual. Since the surprise party yesterday, I've been bombarded with images of my past. And those memories have a bitter taste that yesterday's cake can't mask.

I somehow manage to extricate myself from my pod, even though it feels like my head's a bit foggy—my stomach, too, for that matter. I walk quietly toward the Cafeteria. By this time, there shouldn't be many people left. Hopefully my delay will go unnoticed.

I didn't account for Doc, of course. When I get to the Cafeteria, she's sitting at one of the tables with a tray of unfinished food in front of her. When she sees me coming, she taps the plastic nervously with her fingers.

"Oh, so now you're hungry?" she asks.

Doc has always had a problem with people not following the rules, and she doesn't understand why people break them. For her, duty is an essential trait. I think her attitude is a bit extreme, but it's clear that she's turned out to be a better person than me, so maybe I should try following the rules.

"Sorry. Problem with my alarm clock," I say, improvising.

She brushes my argument aside and hands me an energy-drink box. The straw is already in it.

"Here," she says, pushing the straw up against my visor. "I got this from the machine. No time for a real breakfast. Drink this while we walk."

This isn't really how I wanted to start my day. I would have preferred to sit on my own in a corner, letting myself wake up while eating some leftover cake. Instead, I have to drink something foul while doing my job and trying not to yawn too much.

I groan. But I obey Doc without too much fuss. If there's one thing I am not ready to face in the morning, it's her wrath. There are some battles that are not worth fighting. Any morning argument with Doc is one of those.

"What do you have going on this morning?" she asks, displaying her own schedule on her visor.

"Data to download here and upload in Admin. Calibrating the distributor in Electrical. Then a few tasks at the Reactor and in Security," I reply.

"Perfect! We can do a lot of this together!"

Her sudden enthusiasm is a shift. Well, I'm not going to complain. I decide to follow her graciously while sipping the horrendous drink she gave me.

We start our working day with the closest task. We take turns downloading data from the Cafeteria computer, then uploading it to the one in Admin. It's a bit of a pain, but apparently it's better for IT security. If the computers aren't networked, we can isolate each one if we're attacked and it gets infected, which would keep a virus from spreading. It's pretty basic.

But that means we've got to move things manually. Every day, we move heaps of data from one computer to another, taking a considerable amount of time, only to avoid hypothetical computer attacks by hypothetical pirates. But rules are rules, and I said I'd try to follow them, so I shouldn't start by criticizing them.

The first download in the Cafeteria takes so long that I regret not having negotiated a more substantial breakfast. I'm sure I'd have time for one, but I don't want to annoy Doc.

Once we've both collected our data, we head to Admin. It's really close, so we don't bump into anyone on the way. While we upload the data, which seems to go even more slowly, Doc leans against the dash while I sit staring at the progress bar on the screen.

"Hey, V, can I ask you a personal question?"

"Go ahead," I say, keeping my eyes on the screen.

"Why did you decide to become crew? Considering what happened to your fathers."

I'm glad that she can't see my expression.

When I manage to regain my composure, I turn to her. "I think . . . I just wanted to know."

"Know what?" she asks.

"What about this job was so fascinating that they spent most of their time doing it rather than being with me."

"Oh . . ." Doc's voice cracks.

After a long, quiet moment, she breaks the silence. "So?"

I raise an eyebrow, not really understanding the question.

"Do you know now?"

"There are mornings when I wake up thinking that it's a real blessing to have different galaxies and stars on the horizon with each passing day. And then, sometimes, I feel like this routine is slowly killing me."

"You could ask to be posted somewhere other than a patrol vessel," Doc says. "On a scout, for example."

"Oh no! That would be too stressful."

Doc lets out a loud laugh. "You have to know what you want, V! You can't really escape the routine without trading it in for a dose of stress. What could you see yourself doing, then?"

"I don't know. There are plenty of jobs at MIRA HQ that might be a little more fun. Ones that wouldn't have me putting my life in danger."

"Like what?"

"I . . . I . . . well, it's just an idea. I hadn't really thought it through."

"Hmm, okay."

The discussion ends there, not because we have nothing more to say, but because Janelle and Livia enter the room.

"Hiiiiiiii!" Janelle exclaims cheerfully.

"Data to load?" Doc asks.

"Yep," Livia replies.

"You're going to have to wait in line," I say.

Behind the visor of her red helmet, Livia grimaces. Janelle, on the other hand, looks pretty happy. She takes it as an opportunity to stop and chat without breaking any rules.

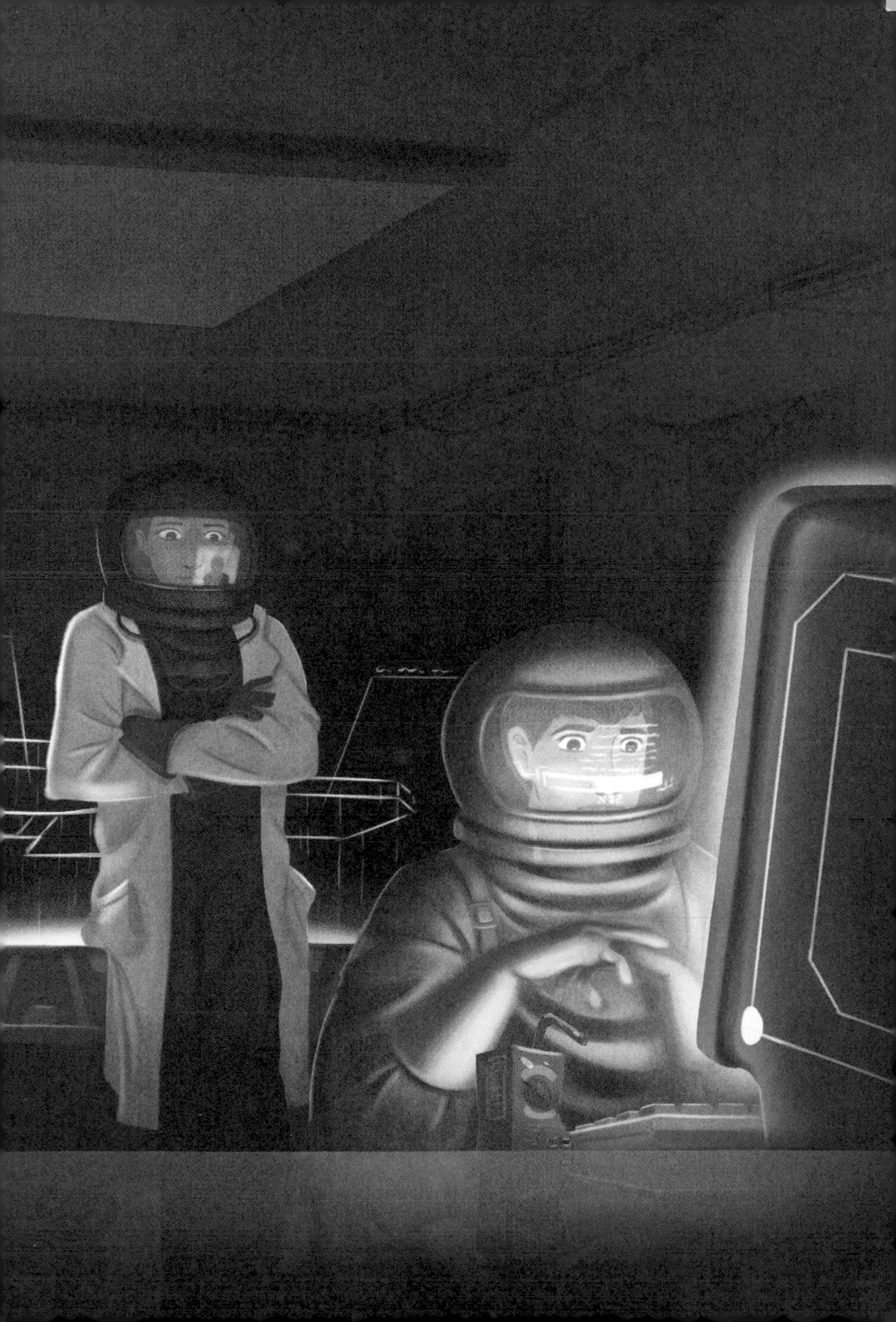

She hops up next to Doc and looks over at me. "So, V, in retrospect, how about that surprise?"

"Quite the performance. I'll give you that."

"Oh! I'm so glad! Did you know I was the one who had the idea to sound the alarm? The lights were JC's idea. I've got to admit that was impressive. Doc just wanted us to send you a message. We had to fight to convince her to make it a little more fun!"

"Fight? That's a bit of a stretch," says Doc, trying and failing to defend herself.

To be honest, that doesn't surprise me. I didn't think Doc would have broken so many rules, even for my birthday. It's even surprising that she let it all happen. I imagine that it was a case of "democracy has spoken" again.

"That was definitely a great idea, Janelle," I say. "But for the sake of everyone's peace of mind, I think it might be good to avoid more of that in the future."

"Don't worry. To be honest, I'd been wondering what kind of noise that alarm would make for days. And now I know!"

"Your download is finished," Livia suddenly says, her voice cold.

Sometimes I don't get what they see in each other. Janelle is an eternal optimist. She's always smiling. She's always welcoming and personable. Livia . . . she's quite the opposite. I don't know if it's due to intense shyness or excessive cynicism, but she's clearly not a big talker. Not that I'm complaining.

I like silence too. But when she speaks to me, I always get the impression she's yelling at me. And that's no fun.

I bet she's different in private. Or maybe that's exactly what Janelle likes. Who knows? I'm not much of an expert on romantic relationships.

Doc and I leave Admin to go to Electrical. In the hallway, we see JC going straight for the Cafeteria. He's walking fast and doesn't see us. When we pass through Storage, we come across Raymond and Alice Stark-Liu in their orange and cyan spacesuits. Like Janelle and Livia, these two are always together. We greet the father and daughter duo and continue on our way.

After we leave the room, Doc shakes her head vigorously without saying a word.

"What's going on?" I ask.

"It's the Stark-Lius."

"What's wrong with the Stark-Lius?"

"You think it's okay for them to bring their kid with them on every mission?"

"Oh, come on. She's not really a kid. She's at least sixteen."

"Fourteen, and just."

"That's what I'm saying. She's a teen, not a little kid."

"I checked in their profile. She's been coming with them practically since she was born. And, whatever her age, it's still problematic. It's really dangerous to have kids here. You have to watch them constantly. They do stupid stuff. Not to mention how draining it is on the parents. Can you imagine if everyone did that? It would be unlivable!"

"I would have liked to have gone with my parents on missions."

Doc stops in her tracks. "V, I'm sorry. That's not what I meant."

"Of course that's what you meant."

I speed up to get away from her. But she takes a few quick steps to catch up with me and grabs my arm.

"V, I'm sorry. I didn't mean to . . ."

I shake my arm free from her grasp. "Drop it. I understand."

I keep going and don't look back. She stays there behind me.

"I'm going to go and check the engines. I'll see you later," I say.

"See you later," she mutters.

Chapter 4

A few days after my birthday, life on the *Skeld* is back at cruising speed. The only difference is that I've been avoiding Doc. I still haven't processed what she said.

I've always seen Doc as a friend, an ally, a confidante, a big sister. It hurt to realize that she thinks children of crew have no place on ships—that they should stay on Polus, away from their parents. I didn't recognize her. For the first time in her company, I felt alone.

She's been making an effort since then, I can tell. It's too soon though. I can't. The thing is, when you're a little impulsive like me, you stubbornly keep your resentments sealed up inside yourself. And it can take a long time to forgive people. It's the first time Doc is on the receiving end of this, and I think it saddens us both. I guess that, somehow, this means we're even?

This is what I'm obsessing about while I try to focus on priming the shields. It's been a long day, and I just want to finish my tasks as quickly as possible, eat a quick meal (I think there's still some cake left), lie down in my bed, and project a good movie on my visor. Something very straightforward, cliché, something to help me completely unplug my brain while watching. That's just what I need! I've been thinking about it since this morning.

When there is no red left on the shield monitor, I breathe a sigh of relief. Okay, just two more tasks and I'm done for the day. I check my map one last time to optimize my trip and memorize the way to my next location. I should print the thing out. The number of times I've gotten lost today! I can't keep doing this.

Well, at least this journey doesn't look that complicated. I have one task left in Navigation, and one in Weapons. I'll do them in that order. It's good that they're close to each other. And after that, I'll be next to the Cafeteria. Perfect! I step out into the hallway, happy to be nearly done with my tasks. I was particularly productive today, despite getting lost. That's good. I'll be able to . . .

UNH UNH UNH UNH UNH

Again?

This is just like the other day when the emergency alarm blasted at full volume throughout the ship.

I automatically place a hand in front of my visor. I'd forgotten how bright that flashing light was. It blinds me for a few seconds, disorienting me. Is it someone's birthday today? They could have warned me! I'm a bit annoyed by all this—I'm going to be running late, and I won't be able to watch a movie at this rate. I drag my feet on my way to the Cafeteria.

Straight ahead to Weapons, then left. I don't see anyone on the way there. I must be the butt of the joke again. Why bother rushing?

Then, suddenly, I hear footsteps from behind me approaching at high speed. I turn around.

It's Doc.

"What's going on?" she asks.

"I don't know. Another birthday maybe. Is it yours?"

"No. Well, I don't think so. . . ." she hesitates. "No, no, it's in four months."

We stay there for a few seconds, looking at one another. I narrow my eyes at her. She's got to be kidding me.

"How about we hurry?" she suggests, clearly embarrassed by my staring.

She takes the lead. I follow, ranting silently to myself.

When we get to the Cafeteria, most of the crew's already there.

"Damn it . . . Janelle . . . this is too much! You promised to stop!" I yell, panting.

"This isn't me! I swear! Baby, tell them."

Livia is about to speak, but JC interrupts.

"Is everyone here?" he asks, his voice cold.

Everyone looks around the room.

"Ray's not here," Juihan says.

JC gives her an odd look. He sighs and says, just above a whisper, "He's not coming, Juihan."

Everyone is watching JC and Juihan silently. What is going on? Where's Raymond?

Flavius is the first to break the silence. "Where is he? Are we throwing a surprise thing for him too?"

Everyone looks embarrassed. Flavius shrugs and looks at JC in confusion. Then it starts to sink in. Juihan screams and sobs, pulling her daughter closer.

"You mean . . ." Doc starts. She can't seem to finish her sentence.

JC finishes for her. "Raymond is dead."

"Oh," says Flavius, looking ashamed.

"Are you sure?" Henry asks.

"Couldn't be more certain."

"What happened?" Livia asks.

"Where is he? Where is he?! Let me see him!" Juihan pounces on JC.

Janelle and I each grab an arm to try to control her. Behind the visor of her green helmet, tears stream from her eyes, her face distorted by incomprehension and anger. She pulls away from us suddenly and runs to the nearest door. But it doesn't open.

"Nobody is leaving here," JC orders.

"Then tell us what's going on!" Livia looks angry.

Meanwhile, Janelle and Flavius are doing their best to calm Juihan. My eyes are drawn to Alice in her little cyan spacesuit. She's just standing there quietly. She hasn't moved. Doc is kneeling in front of her, talking to her, I think.

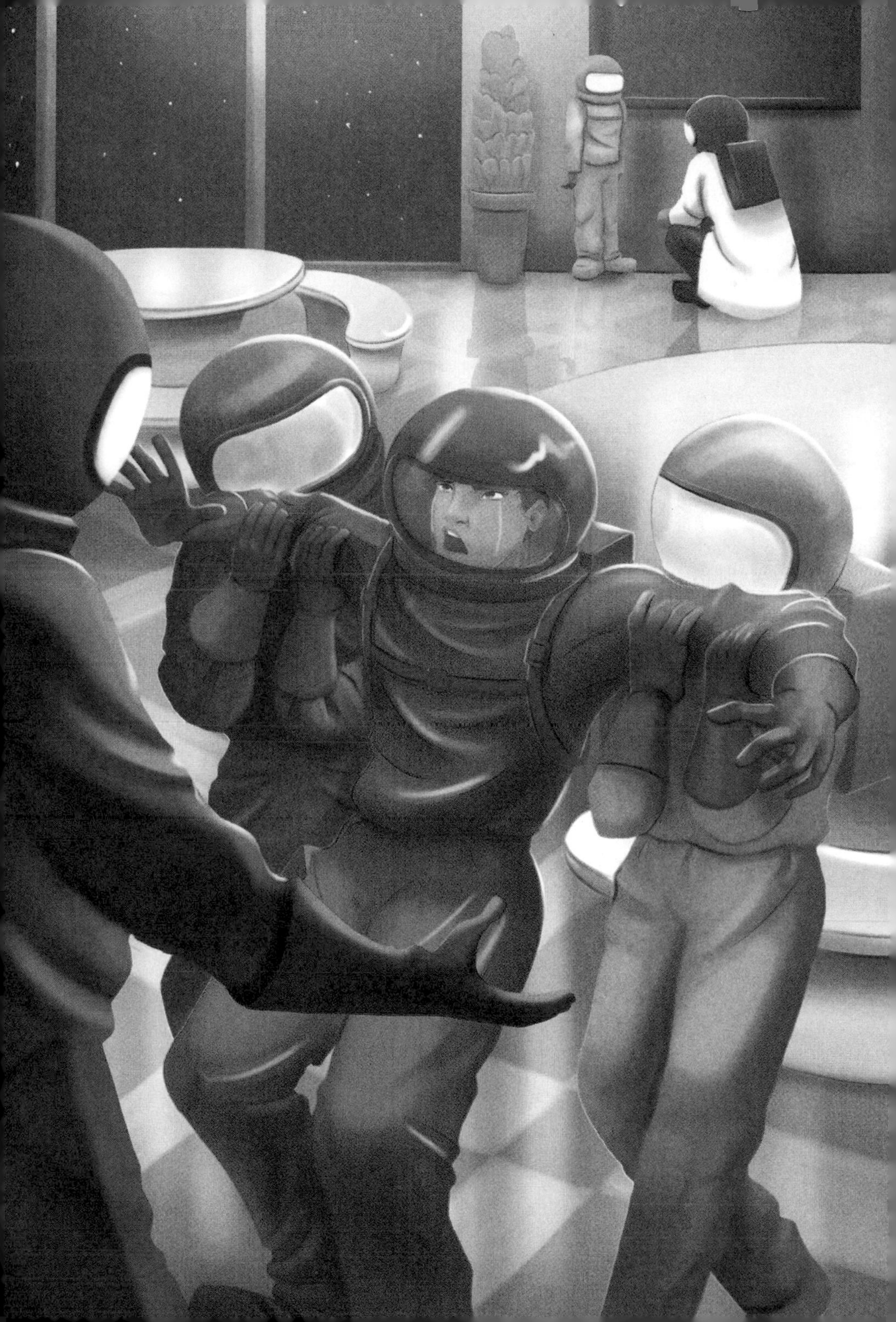

Alice doesn't seem to be listening. She's not even looking at Doc. She's just staring straight ahead like she's contemplating the void. I don't know where she is. Probably very far from here, and certainly not with us. It's a feeling I know all too well. It's like your world suddenly falls out from beneath you, and you can't do anything about it because it's too late.

So you don't do anything. You just stay there with your feet on the ground and your mind somewhere else, watching people move around you.

The loud voices of my crewmates force me back to reality. Livia, Henry, and JC are all speaking at the same time. I can't decipher anything.

"Shut up!" Juihan interrupts them all with authority and calm.

She has dried her tears, and even though her eyes are still puffy, they no longer shine with the same rage as before.

"JC, you're going to tell us everything you know. What happened to him?"

"I don't know what happened. What I do know is that it wasn't an accident." He pauses before continuing. "I . . . I found his body. In such a state . . . he couldn't have done this on his own. Not even with a machine or something. Whatever happened to him, it wasn't natural."

"What do you mean, not natural?" Flavius asks.

"You mean there's a damn murderer among us?" Livia yells.

"I don't know, Liv! As soon as I saw him, I panicked. I've called you all here because that's what the rules say we have to do."

"The rules?" Flavius says.

"What do the rules say?" I ask.

All eyes are on Doc.

"What exactly do you want to know? There are plenty of guidelines in the regulations in the event of death during a mission. Known virus, unknown virus, natural death, homicide . . ."

Everyone is looking at her in confusion at this point.

"Okay, let me explain."

Doc details the contents of the procedure sheet for a homicide on the vessel. The crew must all meet as soon as possible after the discovery of the crime or the corpse. Gathered in council, they must discuss and decide on the plan to follow. As with all decisions, each crewmate has one vote if a proposal is put to a vote. "However, if a culprit is identified, the procedure is very clear."

"And that is?" Janelle asks, looking concerned.

"The murderer is ejected."

"Ejected?" exclaims Henry.

"Without a proper trial?" Flavius looks shocked.

"The crew's decision is the trial," says Doc.

"I can't believe there's a procedure in place for this kind of thing! That's really creepy," says Flavius in disgust.

"Realistic, I'd say," adds Livia.

"So is that what we're gonna do? Suspect each other until someone cracks or we choose to eject a potentially innocent person into space?"

"These are the rules, Janelle," Doc says.

"Then the rules are bullshit!" I say.

Everyone turns to face me.

"What? I agree with Janelle. We can't just toss a coin!"

JC cuts me off. "It's not a coin toss."

"Let's call MIRA! Let them handle it. The trial, the investigation . . ."

"They won't," JC sighs. "I called them. I tried several times. Communication with the outside is down. Nobody's answering. We are on our own."

"Seriously?! Who even made up this damn rule?!"

"Calm down, V," Doc says. "Fighting won't help."

"And where were you all?" Livia asks accusingly.

"Sorry?" Henry chokes out.

"You heard me just fine. I want to know where all of you were before you came here. If you want, I'll start. Janelle and I were in Navigation. We haven't left each other's side all day. Your turn."

"I refuse to take part in this shi—"

"I was in Communications," Doc interrupts me. "V was in Shields."

"And how do you know that?" I bark at her.

"I . . . I followed you from afar for a good part of the day. I was hoping to talk to you, to apologize."

"But . . ." I begin to say.

I'm cut off again, by Livia this time. "Okay. And everyone else?"

"In Storage," Flavius says.

"Alice, what about you? You're normally with your father."

"Livia, you can't be serious!" Juihan is angry. "Are you saying my own daughter is a suspect in her father's murder?"

"I didn't say that."

"She spent the day with me," Juihan says. "We were in Electrical when the alarm went off."

"Good, thanks. Henry?"

"I was here in the Cafeteria. JC can confirm it. I was here when he set off the alarm."

"That's true. I was coming from MedBay. That's where I found the body."

A short silence follows.

"Very well. If I sum up, Janelle and I are each other's alibis. Doc is V's, although no one can confirm that she was really there. The fact that you arrived together doesn't prove a thing. Juihan and Alice haven't left each other either. That leaves Flavius and Henry without alibis, and JC, of course."

"You've got to be kidding me, Livia!"

"I'm just following protocol, Flavius."

"Why would JC have summoned us if he'd killed Raymond?" Janelle asks.

"So we assume he's innocent, just like you're doing," Livia says.

"Just stop. Can you even hear yourself? We're not going to do that!" I yell.

"It's the protocol, V. We have no choice," Livia says. She turns to Doc.

"She's right. . . . It's the rule."

It's like I'm being stabbed in the gut for the second time in just a few days. It's starting to happen a lot with someone I thought was my friend.

"Well, JC, say something!" I yell.

"I can't. She's right. This is an emergency. And with no news from MIRA, we have no alternative: we have to stick to the protocol. We have to vote. Now."

"But you can't just eject someone like that!" Janelle is clearly panicking.

Henry points at Livia. "You're very quick to accuse us. What are you hiding?"

"I swear I didn't do anything! Don't eject me!" Flavius sobs.

"Voting is open," Doc says. "You have two choices: you can nominate someone or pass."

A projection appears on our visors with photos of all the crewmates. Raymond's is blurred and crossed out. As Doc explained, we have the option of clicking on any of our faces to pick the person we think is guilty, or not to pick anyone at all. The choice is ours, and we have to do what we believe is right.

I don't dare touch my helmet in case I accidentally click on someone.

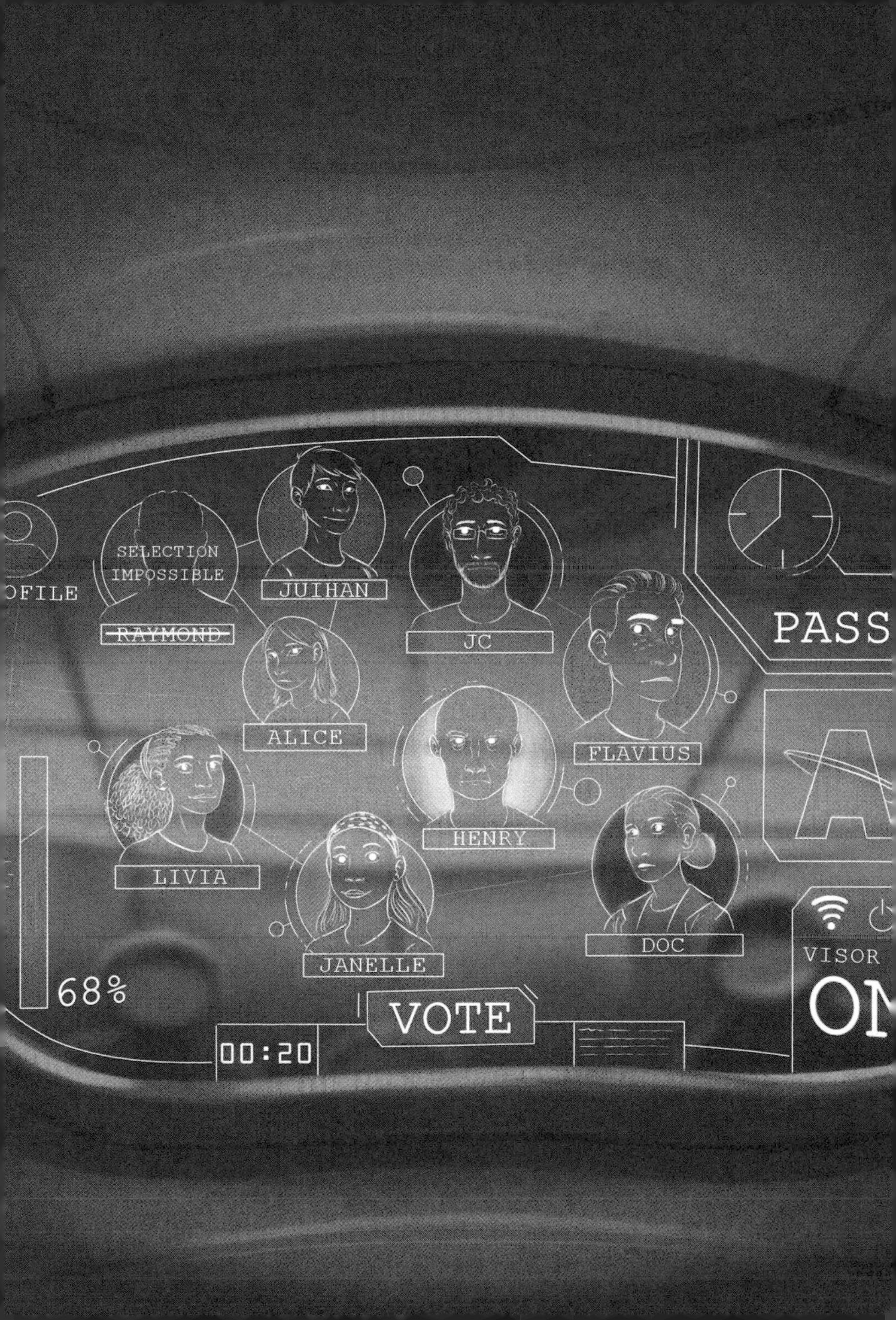

OFILE
SELECTION IMPOSSIBLE
RAYMOND
JUIHAN
JC
ALICE
FLAVIUS
PASS
HENRY
LIVIA
JANELLE
DOC
VISOR
ON
68%
VOTE
00:20

"What happens if we all pass?" Janelle asks.

"No one is ejected," Doc answers.

"Oh! So that's what we have to do!" Janelle exclaims.

"And let a murderer roam free?" Livia retorts cynically.

"There's only five seconds left to vote!" Doc says.

I choose to pass. Five seconds later, a loading screen appears on our visors.

CALCULATING RESULTS.

What's going to happen now?

Chapter 5

NO ONE IS EJECTED.

I exhale in relief. The anonymized results of the vote are displayed on our visors. Three of us are in the clear—Janelle, I think, me . . . but who's the third? Henry and JC got two votes each; Flavius got one. The last vote was directed against Livia, who, like all of us, is surprised.

"Someone voted against me? Why?"

"The idea behind anonymous voting, Liv, is that you don't know who voted for what," says JC.

"You voted against me because I put you on the suspect list, didn't you? Out of revenge?" Livia responds.

"I didn't say it was me."

"You didn't say it wasn't either."

"Are we really going to do this?" Janelle says. "Just stop. We're done. It's over. Isn't that right, Doc?"

"The crew's agreed to do nothing for now. So we can go back to our tasks," Doc replies.

Juihan explodes in rage again. "So we leave a murderer to roam free? What are you waiting for? For them to go after me or my daughter next? You have no respect for my husband! None!"

A small group forms around her and tries to calm her down. It's impossible to make out her screams now, her face contorted with anger. Tears are rolling down her cheeks again. Behind her, Alice remains still, staring into space. She hasn't said a word since we heard the news. I'm guessing she was the third person who was in the clear.

While a bunch of the crew tend to Juihan, Livia lashes out at JC and Doc. She doesn't seem to get that we've voted and the matter is closed. She says we shouldn't leave until the culprit's body is ejected into space, as far away from the *Skeld* as possible.

"What's going to happen now? Are we all just going to quietly resume our tasks while waiting to get killed? Hoping someone else dies before us?"

"We're going to investigate," says JC calmly.

"Who's we?"

"Doc will examine the corpse. She can tell us what really happened there and what Raymond died of. That will surely give us some more clues."

"What if Doc's the one who did it?" Livia says.

"I thought you cleared me earlier."

"Not 100 percent. I still think you're all suspects. And I'm going to carry something I can defend myself with."

JC shakes his head, ignores Livia's remark, and clears his throat. "Doc and I are going to study the body in MedBay.

I don't want anyone around, okay? The MedBay tasks can wait. And while we do that, keep working. Work in groups of two so that we have an eye on everyone."

"I'm new here," Flavius says. "How do you determine who pairs up?"

JC shrugs, visibly annoyed.

"Juihan and Alice obviously can't get back to work," Janelle says.

"I'm going to stay with them for a while," Henry suggests. "I'll make them some food then walk them back to their beds."

"If you want," JC sighs. "Just try to keep an eye on each other."

Livia sneers. "You don't have to worry about that. Come on, Janelle, let's get out of here."

Janelle gives me one last helpless look before following her girlfriend. JC and Doc leave for MedBay, and the Cafeteria gradually empties out. Henry is sitting in a corner with Juihan and Alice. He's trying to talk with them, to reassure them.

Is it really a good idea to leave them both alone with someone who has been clearly identified as a potential suspect? I have always considered Henry as the crew grandfather, not very dangerous, but now . . . I'm starting to doubt that.

"Well, it looks like we're teaming up, partner!" Flavius smiles broadly, his hand reaching out to shake mine. I don't take it, and he ends up removing it abruptly.

"Do you think we should leave Henry alone with the Stark-Lius?" I ask.

"Yeah. Why not? Henry's a nice guy."

"What if he's the killer? He doesn't have an alibi."

"Oh, that . . . huh." He pauses, tapping his finger on the bottom of his helmet at chin level. "Well, if I were the killer—and let me clarify: I'm not—I think that I'd try to keep a low profile. I mean, since we already suspect Henry, it wouldn't be very smart for him to kill the rest of the family after telling everyone he was staying with them, right?"

That makes sense, I think.

"Good. Let's proceed, new partner. What tasks do you have left?"

"Hmm . . . Navigation . . . and a task in Weapons," I say while checking.

"Okay. I've also got a thing in Navigation. Then Storage, the Reactor, then the Upper Engine."

"All that?"

"Yes."

"What the hell have you been doing all day?"

"Hey! I'm new! And all these things are so fiddly. I often have to do each one several times and . . ."

"Okay."

"Hang on."

"What?"

"Do you suspect me?" he asks, looking worried.

"No. I just said okay."

"You sure?"

"Um, yes."

Silence.

"Okay, should we go?" I ask. "Otherwise, you're going to spend all night finishing your tasks, and I don't really want to stay up with you."

In the hallway, we don't say a word. We must both be replaying the past few hours in our minds. If you pushed me, I'd admit that I'm still in shock. I don't have a huge number of missions under my belt, but a murder on board is a big first. I'd never even heard of such a thing.

There are so many rumors at MIRA, urban legends, but they're mostly stories to scare new recruits. It's a kind of rite of passage like anywhere else. I never paid much attention to them. But maybe I should have.

Dying on a ship is obviously something that I'd thought of. I know it happens. I mean, that's what happened to my fathers. But my parents died in a context that I would describe as . . . normal? Well, they died in a battle with the enemy. They weren't soldiers, only crew on a scout, but at the time, that was a known risk. This is space colonization. We gain ground, but we lose people. As long as we emerge victorious, the human losses are just collateral. Like they were just part of the plan.

Death on a patrol vessel these days isn't as common. We no longer intervene. If we see something suspicious, we contact a brigade ship. It's their duty to stop pirate ships and smugglers or to battle an enemy fleet. Sometimes the patrol ships are attacked by aliens, of course. But it's not common. These days, if enemy forces manage to enter the perimeter we cover, it's because scouts didn't do a good job.

That's why I signed up for patrol: these are the safest missions. Of all the jobs involved in the conquest of space, it's one of the safest. And that sounded good to me. Until today, that is.

A murder. In cold blood. Likely premeditated. And quite bloody, going from what JC said. It's enough to make your hair stand on end. I knew there was something wrong with this ship right from the start. I should have trusted that feeling and never boarded. Now it's too late.

I'd like to think this was retaliatory, that the murderer, whoever they are, was only after Raymond and that there's no reason for them to strike again. That's what I'm trying to tell myself as I clear a bunch of asteroids from Weapons. *PEW! PEW! PEW!* Seeing them explode is relaxing in a way. The feeling doesn't last all that long though. I keep thinking of what Livia said.

What if she was right? Maybe we should have stayed locked up in the Cafeteria together until we found and ejected the murderer. Maybe our inaction means we all signed our death warrants. I gulp. Who could have killed Raymond? And why? I think he was a popular guy. I can't see why someone would have murdered him. Okay, so maybe he often ate more than his fair share. . . . But that's not enough of a reason. According to Liv, the only three who don't have an alibi are JC, Henry . . . and Flavius.

Suddenly, Flavius clears his throat.

"Hey, can you hurry up a bit, V? I still have a lot of tasks to do afterward."

"Yeah, yeah, I'm coming. Chill. Just, um, two more and I'm done."

"Okay, fine."

I feel a drop of sweat beading on my forehead when I suddenly realize I'm alone with Flavius. A suspect. A potential murderer. He's right behind me, and I have no idea what he's doing. He could . . . He could just decide to kill me right now. I wouldn't even see it coming. It would be over in just a few seconds, maybe a few minutes. I mean, nobody really knows this guy. He just finished his training. This is his first mission. What if he's a member of a terrorist organization and joined this crew for the sole purpose of sabotaging the mission from within? What if he's an impostor—an impostor among us?

I hurry and finish my task, then jump up, all alert, ready to fight. If he decides to kill me, I won't make it easy for him!

He's leaning against the wall, his arms crossed. He looks at me, dumbfounded. "What's the matter with you, man? Did you see a ghost?"

"No, no. It's nothing. . . . Just, um, it's hot, isn't it?"

"I don't know. About average. Can we go now?"

I nod and follow him through the hallways. I'm keeping my eyes peeled now. There is an impostor, and I need to unmask them as soon as possible if I want to stay alive.

Chapter 6

After finishing our tasks in Navigation, we head for Storage. Janelle and Livia come out just as we get there. The four of us exchange quick nods, but we don't say anything. Flavius and I know that Liv could use anything we say against us. Janelle isn't smiling, which is unusual. She doesn't say anything, but when our eyes meet, she shrugs apologetically.

In Storage, Flavius rushes to fill up his can, and then we go to refuel the Upper Engine. He makes a mess and gets fuel everywhere, but at least he finishes quickly. We don't waste any time and head for the Reactor next.

The hallways are deserted. Flavius starts a conversation and breaks the oppressive silence.

"I can't believe what happened," he says.

"Yeah."

"It's unreal. A murder! Does this happen often?"

"Not really, no."

"I wonder what the probability of this happening on my first mission was! I bet it wasn't high."

I know what you mean, Flavius. What a strange coincidence. I keep these thoughts to myself though. It's better if Flavius doesn't know I suspect him.

"I've been thinking about this for a while. I mean, I wonder who could have done this. Don't you?" asks Flavius.

"Yes, I do."

"And, suddenly, I thought . . . well, nobody mentioned it, but I think it's possible."

"What's that?"

"I was thinking that, maybe, it could be Doc. Like, I mean, she's a brilliant woman, doing some advanced biomedical stuff I don't even understand. And for her internship at the end of her degree, she ends up on this rotten old ship. It's fishy, isn't it? What kind of biomedical stuff is there to do up here? So that's it. I don't get it. But maybe I'm missing something. What do you think? You knew her before this, right?"

"Yeah, we were neighbors when we were kids."

"So?"

"I don't believe it for a second. Doc is an honest and serious woman. I can't see her taking part in anything. She has too much respect for rules to even *think* about doing something like that."

"Well, maybe there are rules we don't know about."

"What do you mean?"

"I don't know. Maybe there's some kind of government experiment or something."

"Oh, come on, Flavius. We're looking for answers, not conspiracy theories."

"Okay, if you say so. Just keep it in mind. You never know."

I stay collected in front of Flavius, but doubt is brewing in me. While I don't think that our leaders are directly or indirectly involved in all this, I've been wondering why Doc is here too. What did she come to study? What part of biomedicine does she even specialize in? She told me about her life, about her studies, but like Flavius, I don't know *exactly* what she's doing here. What is a student of her caliber doing on a rickety patrol ship like the *Skeld*? I'll have to ask her. If she hasn't told me, it's probably because she isn't authorized to. Maybe I'm making too much of it all. I can hardly imagine Doc as a bloodthirsty killer scientist. No, that's completely ridiculous. This whole thing is making me paranoid. And confused. If there's one person I can trust here, it's Doc. At least, I think so.

We quickly arrive at the Reactor where Flavius sits in front of the control panel to start the machine.

A little exhausted by this day that never ends, I lean against the yellow barrier that surrounds the machine and let out a yawn. I'm looking forward to getting to bed tonight. I probably won't even watch a movie after all.

Flavius, as usual, takes a long time to complete his task. I hear him hitting buttons, going back, making a mistake, starting over . . . I'm almost ready to just do it for him so we can finish.

Just as I'm about to ask him to hurry, the ship goes dark. Immediately, the small backup lights come on, and the alarm sounds again. The words "REPAIR LIGHTS" flash in red and yellow on our visors.

"What is that?" Flavius sounds panicked.

"The lights went out. We've got to go fix this."

"Yeah, thanks. I can read. But how do we do that?"

"We have to flip all the circuit-breaker switches. You know, those little signs with the yellow lightning symbols?"

"Sometimes it feels like you think I'm an idiot," he says.

A silence settles between us.

"I was just answering your question," I say.

"And it was a stupid one. Yeah, I know. I tend to lose my grip when I panic, sorry. Okay, let's not waste more time. Follow me."

Somehow, I manage to follow Flavius in the semidarkness. He doesn't seem to have any trouble finding his way. I'm kind of jealous. Although, in theory, it's not that complicated—finding your way while staring at a map and looking for lit signs—at least for people who aren't me.

We quickly repair the first circuit breaker. Flavius's steps are so certain that I can't help but think he knows exactly where the circuit breakers are, even without referring to the map. I mean, who knows every corner of this ship so well that they know where all this stuff is? That's weird for someone new like him, isn't it?

When we flip the switch of the second breaker, the light recovery progress bar displays 80 percent.

"That means the others have been doing their part. There's only one left to fix," I say.

We decide to go to the last circuit breaker. Once there, we find Doc and JC flipping the switch.

Then the light comes back on. My eyes take a few seconds to adjust.

"You're not in MedBay anymore?" Flavius asks.

"We couldn't do much in there without light," JC replies.

"What blew the fuses?" I ask.

"I'm not sure." JC exhales, looking mysterious.

Doc looks like she's about to say something, but we're interrupted by another emergency meeting. The red alarm light flashes violently in my face. I swear, my eyes are getting put to the test today. And I'd hoped to never experience that again. . . . My heart skips a beat.

As the four of us start running toward the Cafeteria, *Who is dead?* is the first question that crosses my mind. Then I look ahead and see Doc. At least it's not her. Then I think of Janelle and worry. On the ship, she's the second person I'm closest to. She's not quite a friend yet, but she's close. Without realizing it, I seem to have lengthened my strides. I hope nothing has happened to her.

When we get to the Cafeteria, I am relieved to see Janelle there, already at a table with Livia by her side. A few seconds after we arrive, Henry, Juihan, and Alice join us. Phew! We're all here. So what is the purpose of this meeting?

Apparently, I'm not the only one wondering. "What are we doing here?" JC asks impatiently.

Janelle takes a deep breath. "I have something to tell you," she says.

"Damn it, Janelle, that button is not a toy!" JC yells.

"You'd better listen to what she has to say," says Livia.

"We're listening," Doc says.

"Earlier . . . before . . . before Raymond's murder. I, um, I saw something." She pauses.

"What did you see?" Flavius asks, seeming a bit defensive.

"I saw Henry. I saw him go through an air vent."

"Sorry?" Henry looks surprised.

"*Go through an air vent*?" JC repeats her words. "What are you talking about?"

"I didn't understand it either. That's why I didn't say anything. Livia and I were going through Shields on our way to Navigation. Henry was there, too, just a few yards ahead of us. When we entered the room from the left, we saw him take the upper hallway. A few seconds later, when we took the same hallway, it was empty."

"What was missing?" Flavius asks.

"Henry! He was gone. We should have seen him since we were going the same way, but he wasn't there. And the air-vent plate was partly open. Then, during the meeting, Henry said it himself: he was already in the Cafeteria when JC arrived! And guess where the air vent in the hallway goes? Directly to the Cafeteria. I'm not saying it was Henry who killed Raymond. I'm just saying his behavior was strange. And I thought everyone should know that."

"Well, now I've heard everything!" Henry exclaims. "You've got quite the imagination, I'll admit, but have you even seen the size of those air vents? No adult, especially not a guy my size, could fit through that. Much less walk there! All this drama has made you lose your mind, my dear."

"He's right, Janelle," says JC. "What you're suggesting is impossible. Henry just walks faster than you, that's all."

"But what about the air vent? Why was it open?"

"I'm sure there's a more logical explanation than 'Henry is traveling *through* the air vents.' Someone might have tripped over it while the alarms were going off and moved it without realizing it, or something."

JC's comment is on target, and everyone seems to agree that Janelle should go get some rest.

Livia, who had not spoken or reacted much before all this, says, "There is something else you should know. After the meeting, Janelle and I went to Admin."

"To do what?" JC asks. "You'd already completed your tasks there, right?"

"Yes. But I thought Henry's behavior was odd, so I wanted to check something out."

"Check what out?" Henry asks, visibly anxious.

"Your file."

Henry doesn't answer, but I have the impression that he's clenching his teeth behind his visor.

"And you found something?" Doc asks.

"Something very interesting," Livia says.

Chapter 7

"Do you know what Henry was doing before he became crew?" Livia asks.

Everyone exchanges glances before shrugging. Everyone has access to all the crew files, but no one tends to look at them. The paperwork is so boring, and we all have so many important things to deal with before and after boarding. And if you read them before you get to know your crewmates, you've spoiled about 80 percent of the conversation topics in the first days of a mission. It's so counterproductive. They're mainly there for nosy people and stalkers. Or, you know, if someone on your ship is murdered.

"Mr. Henry S.," says Livia, "was none other than a famous criminal. Famous for robbing banks. So I wouldn't be surprised if he could get through air vents."

"Henry, is that true?" asks JC.

"Yes. But all that is in the past. It has nothing to do with this. I've served my time. And I never used those damn air vents!"

"We only have your word for that," says Livia. "But maybe Raymond had discovered why you're really here. So tell us, what were you planning to steal?"

"Nothing! Can't you see she's talking nonsense? I'm sure she's been manipulating Janelle. You didn't even see me in

Shields! You made it all up, and you've used my past to incriminate me! I swear: this time, I am innocent."

"This time . . ." JC repeats.

"Why are you getting upset?" Livia asks. "We're just talking."

"You've got to admit that this all sounds suspicious," says Flavius.

All eyes are now on Henry, who looks livid. "You can't be serious!"

"On the contrary, Henry. I am very serious," says Livia. "Who here other than you would have a motive to kill Raymond?"

"Come on! Are you buying what these kids are selling? They're covering for each other! Can't you see it?"

"Why didn't you say anything earlier?" I ask Janelle and Livia.

"At the time, we just thought it was weird. When the alarm went off, we had to react quickly, and we forgot all about it. We didn't make the connection. It was later, after we were talking about it all, that we both realized these things could be linked. So we looked into him. And what we found shows that Henry has stuff to hide," Livia replies.

"This is absolutely ridiculous! I'm not going to stay here another second listening to this nonsense." Henry walks to the door closest to him. But it's locked. "Really? Let me out, damn it!" he yells, punching the door hard.

"It's protocol, Henry," Doc explains, sounding sorry.

Sitting around another table, Alice and her mother watch all this without saying a thing.

They both look so tired. It seems like Juihan aged ten years in a few hours. The situation is terrible, but they are facing it with a dignity that commands respect. I shiver every time I look at them.

It's only a matter of time before the voting screen appears on our visors. And, with it, the countdown. Then we'll only have a few seconds to decide the outcome of this emergency meeting: voting to eject one of us or to maintain the status quo for a while longer.

My heart is racing in my chest. On one hand, this voting thing is so stupid. I'm not a fan of deciding the fate of one of our crewmates spontaneously, like some kind of people's court. It's uncivilized. It's like a lion's den. Livia has just thrown Henry to the ground in front of everyone.

But on the other hand . . . what they found is disturbing. A former criminal is on board our ship. We've got an imposter to find. . . . Henry could have at least mentioned it. But he didn't. Personally, I believe in second chances. But I wish Henry had been honest with us from the start. I wish he had laid his cards on the table so we knew what to expect. The fact that he hid his past from us does make him a bit suspicious.

But does he deserve to have everything bad happening on this ship pinned on him? Being a thief doesn't necessarily make him a murderer. The connection is a little weak.

Around me, the others seem to be plagued by the same doubts. Janelle, who was so fiercely opposed to ejecting one of us, now seems inclined to kick Henry out as quickly as possible. Could Livia have manipulated her to her own ends?

Flavius also seems torn. I think he has the same concerns I do. Except that he's also one of the suspects. Somehow, Livia's scathing accusation against Henry is working. He's pale as a ghost. JC is too. So I decide to make a point. We shouldn't be making this kind of decision on a whim.

"We only have one suspect then, if I understand correctly?" I say.

Henry glares at me.

"It seems pretty obvious," says Livia.

"I don't know. Earlier, you listed three suspects. More if you consider that you weren't fully convinced of Doc's innocence. And you even suspected the Stark-Lius. Now you're certain it's Henry?"

"Come on, V. Are you stupid or something? Henry has a motive. The others don't."

"Yeah, I know. That's what you've been saying. But just because Henry *has* a motive doesn't mean that the others don't."

"Sorry, detective, I'm not following you," JC says.

"The kid is just trying to tell you that my conviction would suit *some people* here," Henry says. "I might be a former thief. And let's say, by some miracle, I managed to use an air vent to get around—that doesn't prove anything. You say you saw me in Shields before I got to the Cafeteria using the air vent.

But the murder took place in MedBay, on the other side of the ship. JC was in MedBay. What a coincidence."

"I discovered the body!" the man in the black spacesuit yells.

"Of course. But who says you're not the one who put him there?" Henry asks.

"That makes no sense! You're trying to shift the suspicion onto us, Henry, and it's pathetic. Everything points to you, old man," JC says.

"And what about Flavius? Huh?" Henry is clearly losing his temper. "Where was he? What was he doing? Have you ever seen him tweak things he shouldn't be touching? Because I have! Doesn't the time it takes him to do each task seem suspicious to you as well? And if I'm not mistaken, Storage isn't that far from MedBay if you go through the Cafeteria. Who says he isn't the murderer?"

I have to admit that he's not completely wrong. I've noticed Flavius's suspicious behavior myself. He knows the ship's map like the back of his hand, but he can't do a simple task without it taking forever? That just doesn't sound right.

"And the others? Why aren't the others suspects? Livia and Janelle are always together. That suits them, doesn't it, to be able to exonerate each other every time? And Valdemar, what about him? He's always wandering aimlessly, then suddenly turning around in the hallways. This guy keeps getting lost in the ship after three weeks? Come on. I don't buy it."

Come on, man. You're digging your own grave. To think I almost gave him the benefit of the doubt. And he blames me when I've tried to defend him? That's not a good strategy.

Just then, the voting screen is displayed, triggering the countdown.

"You are pathetic, Henry," says Livia. "Just admit to it. It'll be easier for everyone."

"I will never confess to a crime I didn't commit, you little . . ." Henry rushes across the room to pounce on Livia.

Juihan gets in his way. "What did you do to my husband?" she screams, full of rage. "Why? What did he do to you?"

Doc and I rush over to separate them before they come to blows.

"There are only ten seconds left to vote," Livia says both calmly and cynically.

For a few seconds, I hold Henry with one hand so I can vote with the other . . . *10, 9, 8* . . . Even if everything points to him, I can't click on his photo . . . *7, 6, 5* . . . Even if he were guilty, it's another thing entirely to sentence him to death in the cold void of deep space. It's a line I can't cross . . . *4, 3, 2, 1* . . .

CALCULTING RESULTS.

The verdict is final.

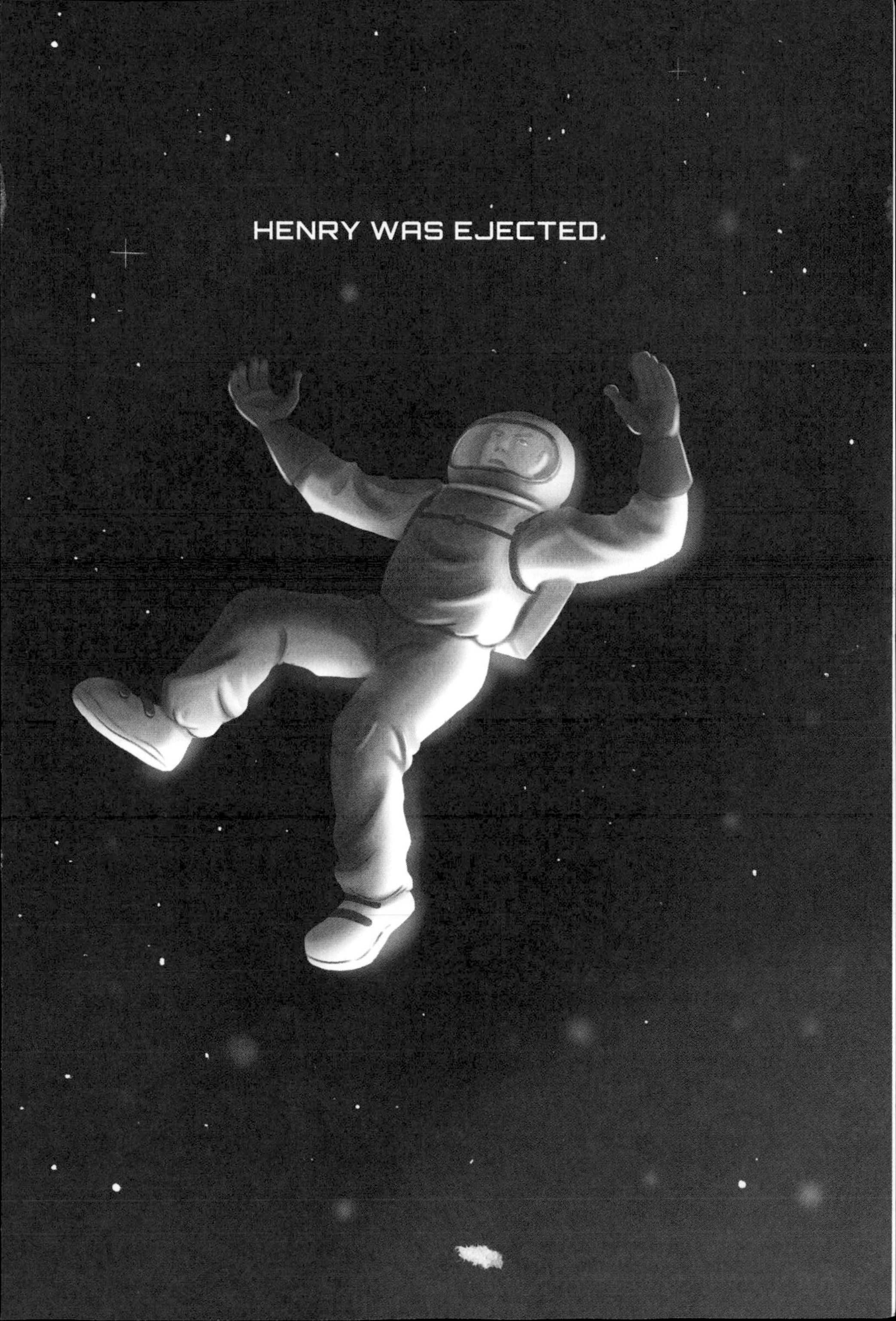
HENRY WAS EJECTED.

Chapter 8

After Henry is ejected, everyone takes off to complete their tasks as quickly as possible. We leave in the groups that JC recommended. But aside from Janelle and Livia, everyone goes about doing their tasks alone.

In my sleeping pod, I remove my spacesuit. I lie on my back and stare up at the metal ceiling. I don't want to put on my headphones to watch a movie, but I don't think I can sleep either. With everything that's happened today, my head is spinning. It's all playing over and over in my mind. Just this morning, everything was normal. And in just a few hours, we plunged into a nightmare.

I hope I wake up tomorrow morning and realize that this has all just been a bad dream, something I came up with from playing too many video games. I sigh. Of course, it's all very real, much too real. We are so far from the quiet, uneventful mission I had hoped for. Now I'm certain: if I make it out of this alive, my spacefaring days are over. I'll find an office job, anything, even a Cafeteria or cleaning job at MIRA. Or I'll leave everything and go to farm some land in a remote corner of Polus. There are lots of options. I just have to survive, and I'll have new opportunities.

Until then, I decide to be smart about how I handle all this. I'm going to keep a low profile and stay alert. If Henry was actually the murderer, the nightmare might be at an end. But if he wasn't . . . well, I'd rather be careful than end up with a dagger stuck in my back because I wasn't paying attention. After several hours of fine-tuning my survival strategy and imagining my life after the *Skeld*, I finally fall asleep.

The next morning, I wake up groggy with an excruciating migraine. Hopefully breakfast will be enough to help it pass.

The Cafeteria is already very busy when I arrive. Janelle, Livia, Flavius, Alice, and Juihan are already there, seated at three different tables.

"Hi," I say to the room.

Flavius waves, and Janelle just looks up. And those are the only answers I get. Okay, I guess that's what this morning is going to be like. Annoyed, I decide to go and sit alone at the table in the middle of the room. It's got a stack of toast on it that could compete with the MIRA HQ tower. I might not have company at breakfast this morning, but at least I won't starve! There's a heavy, strange, quiet atmosphere as we all eat.

Suddenly, the door slams. JC and Doc enter the Cafeteria together in silence.

JC looks around the room before asking, "Is everyone here then?"

Nobody answers.

"Perfect," he continues. "Doc and I have something to tell you. It's about Raymond's death."

The toast I was holding is suddenly on the floor. Jam-side down, of course. But I leave it and, like everyone else, turn to them. JC steps aside, and Doc comes forward and speaks.

Her eyes look shifty, and she seems hesitant. To give herself some composure, she clears her throat a little before starting. "The autopsy of Raymond's body revealed that an unknown virus was responsible for his death."

And I thought the atmosphere couldn't get any heavier. . . . The seconds tick slowly away.

Finally, Flavius says, "Does that mean Henry was innocent?"

"Not exactly," Doc replies.

"What do you mean? I don't understand—if it was a virus that killed him, what does that have to do with Henry?" he asks.

"From my initial findings, it seems that the goal of this virus is not to kill its host, but to develop in it. The virus would not seek to kill, but to infect. So it's possible that Henry was infected and tried to pass the virus on to Raymond, but it didn't work."

"There are a lot of unknowns in your story, Doc," says Livia.

"I haven't finished. I will continue looking into this, and I'll let you know as soon as I learn more."

"And where do you think this virus came from?" Livia continues as though she hadn't even bothered to listen. "The ships are checked and disinfected before each mission. The health policy is very strict on this subject because we know that if there's an infection on board, the spread is fast and . . . complete."

"Thank you, Livia," JC interrupts. "I think Doc knows the subject at least as well as you do."

"It doesn't sound like it," Livia says.

"Liv, please," Janelle begs her. "Keep going, Doc."

"Livia is right: MIRA's protocols in the event of an epidemic are very strict. That's why we're going to ask all of you to follow a number of new rules from now on," says JC.

"What kind of rules?" Flavius asks.

"I'm getting to that."

JC then launches into the new protocols to avoid the spread of the virus, admitting that it's still on the ship despite Henry's ejection. According to him, these measures are above all preventative.

So, starting this very minute, we now have to: eat our meals alone, systematically lower our visor in the presence of another team member, maintain a safe distance of at least three feet between us, avoid extended gatherings and discussions with one or more crewmembers, and regularly disinfect our spacesuits and shared equipment.

"From now on," JC says, "I don't want to see you systematically walking in pairs."

"It's ridiculous!" Livia yells. "And above all: it won't be enough."

"This may help slow the spread until we find a solution," JC replies.

"What kind of solution?" Livia says.

"A treatment, for example. Or something else."

"What do you mean, *something else*?" I ask.

"If Doc finds a way to detect the presence of the virus in our bodies, we can . . . *get rid* of the infected."

"What a nice word to describe murder!"

"I guess I don't understand you very well, Livia," says JC. "Yesterday you didn't really seem to care all that much about 'murdering' Henry." JC uses air quotes when saying "murdering."

"That was different."

"How so?"

"I thought Raymond's death was a cold-blooded murder. Not anything to do with a virus," says Livia.

"Oh, I see, and in that case, arbitrary execution was okay?" JC asks.

"If it's a virus, couldn't we look for a cure instead?"

"Nice change of subject, Livia!"

"Back off, JC!"

"I doubt I can find a cure in such a short time with such limited equipment. Maybe I can identify the virus, but eradicating it is another story," Doc says with regret.

"So you're no longer in favor of votes and ejections, Livia?" JC won't drop it.

"Are you doing this on purpose or something?! Can't you see the difference? If the murder was the work of a single person, yes, ejecting them from the ship fixed the problem. But if it's a virus . . . shit, JC, that means we could all be infected, sooner or later, and not even know it. So, yes, that does change things *just a little*," Livia says.

The sound of her catching her breath is the only noise in the room. We are all quiet. Her point hit home. We are all beginning to realize what Doc's discovery really means. If Henry was the only carrier of the virus, then we are safe. If one of us is infected, then eventually we could all be. At this point, each crewmate looks at one another with suspicion.

"And this . . . this virus, do you know more about how it works, Doc?" I ask.

"Not yet."

"Doc will continue her research in MedBay," JC says. "Her other tasks will be distributed evenly among us. If you need to go to MedBay, for whatever reason, do not disturb her. Is that understood?"

We nod like puppets tied to the same string.

"Does everyone agree with the new rules?" Doc asks.

We all nod again.

"Anyway, if you don't, you know what you are exposing yourself to . . ."

I gulp. I picture Henry again in the airlock. The features of his face distorted, pleading, just before the airlock opened and sent him into space. Forever. I don't want to be in that situation, and I'm starting to grasp how real this is.

For a few seconds, the Cafeteria is silent again. Then, little by little, there are sounds of chair legs scraping the floor, of the garbage can lid being lifted, of the door being opened, and of footsteps receding.

Everyone returns to their tasks. Or almost everyone. Juihan and Alice haven't moved. They are still just sitting there. Neither of them took part in the argument just now. It's like it's all too much for them, or maybe they don't have much to do anyway. I don't have the guts to go talk to them, so I, too, throw away my leftovers and leave the Cafeteria.

And now my migraine is even worse.

Chapter 9

I lumber through the hallways of the ship, my head feeling like someone's taking a chisel to it. It's going to be a very, very long day.

Skull throbbing with every step, I head toward O2 to clean the filter. When I get there, I can't stop myself from sighing. This task is so annoying. I have to remove dried leaves that have come in through the vents, one by one. My migraine is making it difficult to perform the repetitive motions, and I have to start over several times before I'm done. I am clearly not myself right now. Just like yesterday, all I want to do is dive back into my tube, sleep, and forget everything that's going on here.

In theory, we've got another two months on this mission. With everything going on, we've agreed to turn around and head back toward MIRA to settle all this as quickly as possible. Good idea. I can't imagine living in this noxious atmosphere for two more months. The three weeks that separate us from Polus already sound like an eternity.

These last two days have been particularly trying. And we've got to go through another twenty or so like this? I don't think I can manage. I'm putting all my hopes in Doc. Maybe if she can find out where this virus came from, we can find a way of eradicating it from the *Skeld*. Somehow . . .

The morning crawls by. Our tasks are already pretty boring, and when you add loneliness to the mix, it sure doesn't get any better.

With these new rules requiring us to stay away from each other, we have to keep interactions to a minimum. Now, when I meet someone in the hallways or in a room, we hardly greet each other. Most of the time, we don't even speak. We just exchange a knowing look. Are we really going to live like this until we get home?

I tend to be a solitary person, and I'm already feeling the weight of this isolation. I decide to send a message on the group comm.

V

Hey, it's quiet around here!

Flavius

Haha, man

Janelle

JC

What the hell are you doing, V? Seriously, get back to work. You're already so far behind on your tasks

I don't get any other response to my communication attempt and decide to give up. JC is right. At this rate, I won't wrap up my tasks until midnight. And reading the messages makes my migraine worse anyway. *Come on, V, focus!*

My next task brings me straight to MedBay.

When I enter the room, just for a second, I forget what's going on there now. Then I see large plastic tarps stretched across the room, which remind me that Doc's here . . . with Raymond. I hear the sounds of tools and machinery being used behind that opaque wall. What the hell is she doing to poor Ray? I try not to think about it, to concentrate on my task instead.

But after a few seconds, MedBay is suddenly quiet.

"Hey, V?" Doc peeks out from between the tarps. Her white coat is covered in blood . . . and other stuff I can't and don't want to identify.

"What's up?" I whisper.

"Come over here. I need to talk to you."

"Are you nuts? What if someone sees us?"

"We'll be careful."

I look around, then, resigned, walk over. I'm glad I don't have to raise my visor because I'm pretty sure whatever she's messing with here isn't friendly.

"I've discovered some things," she says.

"What kind of stuff? About the virus?"

"Yes. And I don't think it's a virus, actually."

"What do you mean? What is it then?"

Doc grabs my spacesuit and pulls me through to the other side of the tarps. "I think . . . I think it's alien."

"Alien," I repeat like a zombie.

"Yeah, I know. It's shocking."

Before my half-astonished, half-panicked face, Doc launches into a series of explanations. "When we—I mean us humans—arrived on Polus, it wasn't actually unoccupied."

"What do you mean, 'unoccupied'? You mean the planet was inhabited?"

"Partially, yes. But I'm not talking about the side we first discovered and occupied. To put it simply, only one of Polus's two hemispheres was already inhabited when we landed."

"What are you saying, Doc? Which hemispheres? Half the planet was blown up long before we arrived!"

"Um . . . not exactly."

Doc tells me about the unpleasant surprise the colonists found when they discovered that Polus was not the deserted planet they had imagined. When they were already settled on half of the globe and were planning on bringing the remaining people from Earth to populate the other half, they found local life-forms, and it changed their plans.

A war took place, directly on Polus, between humans and the aliens. It resulted in the annihilation of more than 50 percent of the planet . . . and the indigenous life-forms.

I am stunned. This is not at all the official version of Polus colonization that we're taught at school. I think of Flavius and his conspiracy theories, and I suddenly feel very stupid. I just thought he was kind of a dumbass, but maybe I'm the naïve one.

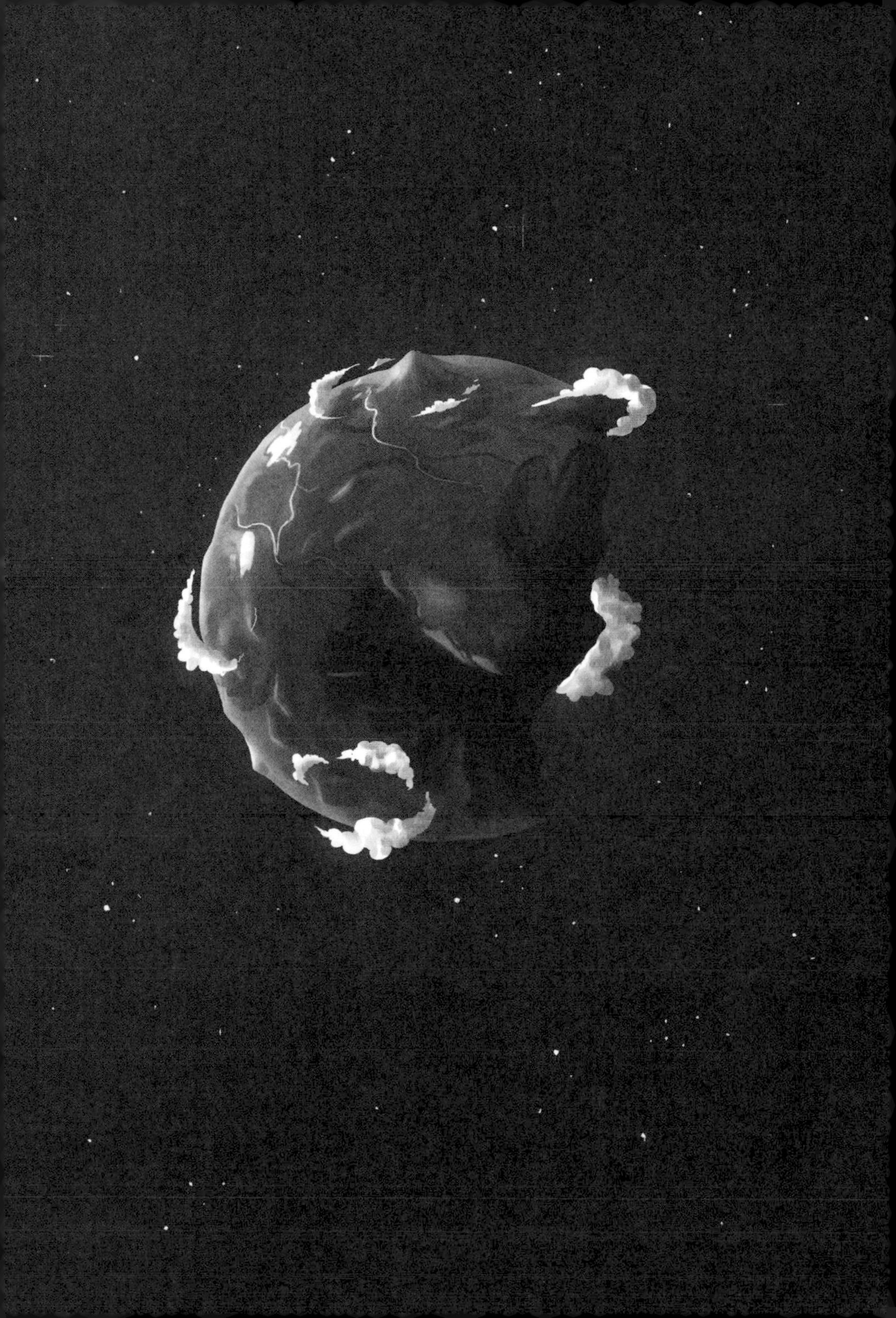

"Does this have any connection with the Great Defense?" I ask her.

"It has everything to do with it. Before Polus partially exploded, some of the aliens who lived there managed to escape on ships. For years, no one heard from them. But when they managed to grow their ranks and reorganize their fleet, they returned, ready to reclaim Polus."

"And we were made to believe that *our* planet was savagely under attack."

"Absolutely. It was important that public opinion embraced the necessity of the war. So we had to pass it off as an external threat for people to fight. And it worked. After a few years, the alien threat was wiped out. It was a great victory for Polus."

At these words, I laugh sarcastically. It wasn't a great victory for everyone. It was during this war that my parents died. I thought they died heroes. Now, I'm not so sure. This planet belonged more to the aliens than to us. My migraine is getting more intense, and I start feeling nauseated.

"Everything okay, V?" Doc asks.

"Yeah, yeah. It's just . . . It's a lot at once."

"I know. Sorry." Doc puts her hand on my shoulder but withdraws it almost immediately.

It's the first time we've really spoken to each other since the incident. Something has clearly changed between us. It's not like it used to be. We're still close, but the warmth is missing. We stand there in silence for a few seconds.

"So what do the native Polusians have to do with Raymond's death?" I ask.

"Well, when I looked things up, I found out that the *Skeld* is an ancient alien ship, a spoil of war, outfitted to suit our needs."

The design flaws suddenly make more sense. "You mean that all this time, aliens have been hiding in this ship . . . just to kill us at the opportune moment?"

"That's the idea, yes. Aliens. Or whatever is left of them."

"But how? Wouldn't they be dead?"

"I don't know yet. That's one of the things I'm still trying to figure out. It's not that simple. We know so little about that life-form. It seems to be much more developed than what we'd originally imagined. It could be that, out of survival instinct, they went into some kind of extreme energy-saving mode and assumed the form of this virus in the hopes of being able to infect another life-form later. But that's just a theory, of course. . . ."

I massage my temples. The pain is increasing by the minute. And all this information I'm trying to digest is not helping.

"Okay . . ." I respond. "So, in summary, we boarded a ship belonging to the aliens whose planet we colonized several decades ago, and one or more of these aliens have, in some way or another, found a way to survive here and infect us . . . or kill us. But what for?"

"Survival, at least."

I let out the longest exhale of my life. "Have you spoken to JC?"

"No, nobody yet. Except you."

"Why?"

"V, we are talking about a highly intelligent entity clearly capable of taking possession of a human body, perfectly imitating its host and infecting us. All of us. At this point, I don't really trust anyone anymore."

I gulp. "And you're telling me about it?"

"It's probably bullshit. But you're the only one I think that I can still trust. Because I knew you before all this."

"Doc?"

"Yes?"

"From what you say, these aliens, they can spread . . . through us. Is that right?"

"That's right."

"So . . . there could already be several among us?"

"It's possible."

Doc is probably right. It's better that this doesn't get out. If the infected crewmate or crewmates know that we know, carnage will surely follow.

And if uninfected crewmates learn about it . . . the result will probably be the same: we'll end up killing one another. Just as I'm about to ask Doc what she's going to do, the door to MedBay opens.

Doc motions for me to stay still and be quiet. You can't really see more than a shapeless mass through these tarps. Hopefully, they can't see the purple of my spacesuit. . . .

"Doc?" JC calls out. "Is everything all right?"

"Yes, why?" she replies, making herself look busy.

"No reason." He pauses. "Actually, no, there is. I was taking a look at the cams earlier, and . . . I saw V heading this way. But I didn't see him come out. Did you see him?"

"V? Maybe. Someone came in to do a task a little while ago. I don't know if it was him. Anyway, they didn't stay long and didn't interrupt me."

"Okay, thanks. I must have missed it on cams. Good luck with everything in there."

A few seconds later, he's gone.

I gesture to Doc to let her know that I'll go too. I don't want anyone wondering where I've been.

She grabs my arm. "Wait," she whispers. "Knowing him, he's probably hiding out in the hallway, ready to catch you as soon as you leave here. Stay a little longer. He'll get bored in a bit . . . especially if he doesn't want to look suspicious."

I nod and obey. The last thing I need is for JC to have it in for me. I let a few minutes pass before leaving MedBay and watch Doc move around behind another tarp, absorbed in her work.

This is the first time since I've known her that I've seen her listen to her gut rather than obey the rules. It makes me shudder. These aliens, how many are already among us? Has Doc told me everything she knows?

Chapter 10

I leave MedBay discreetly. As I walk toward Weapons, I see someone in the hallway. I flatten myself against the wall next to the door to the Cafeteria. I don't want anyone seeing me, especially not JC. He can't know that I've just come out of MedBay.

The footsteps are approaching.

My heart is racing in my chest. When the person is really close, they suddenly turn around and walk away, going back to Weapons.

Intrigued, I decide to come out from my hiding place and quietly sneak down the hallway.

I see Juihan. She is alone. She enters Weapons, then comes out again almost immediately and heads down the hallway, maybe toward Navigation. I decide to follow her. But I have to be careful because a few seconds later she's turned around again. What is she doing?

I try to back up quickly so she doesn't see me.

When I realize that I'm not going to be able to hide, I walk over to her as though I'd just come from the Cafeteria.

"Hi, Juihan. Are you all right?" I ask sincerely.

The sound of my voice makes her recoil. Her response could not be stranger—something's wrong. "Stay away!" she yells.

I obey and stop instantly. She has also stopped.

She stares at me. Her breathing is rapid and choppy.

"Where's Alice?" I ask innocently.

"What's it to you? What do you want with her? Go away!" She yells at me as she approaches, looking menacing.

"Juihan, I have to go to Weapons to perform my tasks."

"I said *leave*. Don't come near me!"

She's only a few steps away from me now. I don't stick around to ask questions. I turn and head straight for the Cafeteria. So much for going to Weapons. I'll have to save that task for last.

In the Cafeteria, I sit at a table and give my heart time to calm down a bit. My head is still a mess. It's like there's an orchestra between my ears, banging and buzzing. I take my head in my hands and close my eyes for a few seconds. Just a little moment of calm. Just time to breathe.

This whole thing is a lot to absorb in such a short time. Doc throwing state secrets at me, JC watching me on cams, Juihan yelling at me . . . I feel like I'm becoming completely paranoid. I have to get some rest. I have to sleep. Everything will be better after I sleep. I just need time to digest all this. *It will be fine, it will be fine, it will be fine. . . .* I repeat it to myself over and over again to try to convince myself.

"V? V? V! Are you okay? Wake up!"

Someone is shaking my shoulder, and it pulls me from sleep. I'm still in the Cafeteria. Janelle is standing in front of me, looking worried.

"What's wrong?" she asks when I lift my tired eyes to her.

"Nothing . . . I just dozed off, I think. Not for long, I swear!"

"That's not what it looks like. Well, whatever, I was looking for you anyway."

"Me? Why?"

"I . . . I want to talk to you."

"I don't know if that's a good idea, Janelle. What if someone sees us? I think JC is watching cams, and maybe he's not the only one."

"They can't keep us from talking for three weeks! Come on, follow me."

"Where are we going?"

"To Admin."

"Why?"

"That way, if someone sees us, I can leave and you can do your task, or pretend to—I don't care. It gives us an alibi."

It all seems a bit sketchy, but I follow her anyway. The concern in her eyes is unusual. Something's going on with her, and I think I want to know what it is, even if it puts us both in danger. Anyway, it's not like there's anything wrong with talking!

Once we reach Admin, I sit in front of the station to upload data. Janelle settles in a little farther away, ready to leave if anyone comes in.

"So, what did you want to tell me?" I ask, my eyes glued to the door.

"It's about Liv," she confesses.

I turn to her then, curious.

Janelle tells me her girlfriend's behavior is getting stranger and stranger, starting with this obsession with trying to prove Henry guilty.

She says it came out of nowhere. Liv didn't hate Henry. And she admits that the vent story was probably more a combination of circumstances than anything else. Even though she agreed with Liv at first about Henry being a criminal liability, she's not so sure anymore. And then there was Liv's change of heart during the last emergency meeting. After being in such a hurry to see Henry ejected, Livia suddenly found the punishment completely disproportionate.

Janelle stops there, but I can tell from her tone, her shifty gaze, and the way she's fidgeting that there's something else. She doesn't seem to want to talk about it, and I decide to not push it. The fact that she's confessed her suspicions so willingly is enough for me.

I think about telling her what Doc told me. It's weighing on me, and to talk about it would do me good. But at the last moment, I change my mind. I know what could happen if I share this, and I can't risk it. Even if her doubts are sincere, there's no way of knowing that she won't turn around and tell Livia everything I say, even if she is suspicious of her. I still decide to play the confession card, too, but by speaking about Juihan.

"I've noticed some strange things too."

"You have? About Livia?"

"No, about Juihan. Have you seen her today?"

"Just briefly in the hallways. We didn't talk, and I didn't stop."

"I saw her behaving really strangely earlier," I confess.

"Strange how?"

"She was going back and forth between Weapons, Admin, and the Cafeteria. She would enter a room, then come back out after a few seconds. She went down a hallway, then suddenly changed her mind and turned around."

"Do you think it was intentional?"

"Maybe."

"But why would she do that?"

"I don't know. Maybe she was waiting for someone. Or she wanted to make it look like she was doing specific tasks."

"Do you think," Janelle hesitates, "that maybe she's just out of it? I mean, she just lost her husband in terrible circumstances. Maybe this is her starting to grieve. It's not like everyone mourns the same way."

"It's possible. But be careful if you have to be alone with her. When I asked her where Alice was, she practically threatened me."

Janelle promises to be careful, and we agree to go our separate ways so as not to arouse any suspicion. She leaves the room, and I wait a few minutes before following her.

When I enter the hallway, I come face to face with JC.

We stop a few feet apart and stare at each other. He doesn't say anything, and neither do I. Is he going to tell me about what he saw on cams? Ask me what I was doing in MedBay?

Finally, he gives me a wide grin, his eyes shining with malice, and continues on his way without saying a word. I go on my way too. On my visor, I display the list of tasks I still have to do and let out a long sigh. I haven't even finished a third of what I have to do today. I'll have to hurry if I want to avoid suspicion.

Despite the still pulsing, still intense migraine, I pick up the pace. As everyone starts to distrust one another, I have to be blameless if I want to be left alone. And that starts with doing my job well and on time. *Come on, V! You've got work to do!*

I promise myself to be on my guard. If what Doc said is true, we're all in danger. We are all *a* danger.

Did Janelle lie to me? Is Livia a threat? What is making Juihan act that way? Where's little Alice? Why is JC watching me? And what is Flavius doing? It's been hours since I saw him. . . .

Chapter 11

Luckily for my head and its ache, the rest of the day unfolds normally, more or less, if you leave out how weird the ship's atmosphere has been since JC introduced his new rules.

The next day, I wake up in my pod feeling refreshed. My migraine is gone. I'd almost forgotten what it was like to move around without it hammering up there. It's the same with every headache. I feel like it will never end, and then it passes; I feel alive again, and then it starts all over. Over and over. This time, I plan on taking advantage of feeling strong. I open my eyes and the door to my pod, and everything seems much clearer than the day before.

It's still very early as I head toward the Cafeteria with determination.

When I get there, it's empty, as I expected. Nobody is awake at this time, which suits me well. I throw back a hearty breakfast at full speed without wasting any time. (There's no cake left anyway.)

I've thought about it, and I've come up with a battle plan for the day ahead. Since we are stuck in here with a virus that can turn anyone into a bloodthirsty killer, I have to come up with a defense strategy, and quickly. Thanks to what Doc told me, I've also got a bit of a head start on my crewmates.

I want to be able to quickly identify the culprit by cross-checking what Doc said and what I've observed. (I really hope that there's only one imposter, although I can't rule out the possibility of there being more.) But to do that, I've got to do meticulous investigative work and be the soul of discretion. It's going to take a lot of time. More time than I've got with all the tasks I have to do on the *Skeld*. So I'm up early. I've got to do as much as I can before the rest of the crew wakes up so I have time to watch and record everything they do without getting caught. Finding motivation I never knew I had, I roll up my sleeves (so to speak) and get to work.

After an hour and a half, I've already completed more than half of my tasks. I'm quite proud, even if my head is spinning from all this running around. It's time to give myself a well-deserved break. I leave Storage and head for Security.

My crewmates are starting to wake up. On my way, I see Janelle, who is coming out of Electrical, and Flavius, who is heading from the Upper Engine to the Reactor.

Each time, we only exchange a brief wave.

I open a blank document on my visor and carefully make a note of the name of the person I pass, along with the time and place I saw them. You never know. If there's an emergency meeting, it could come in handy.

When I get to Security, the room is empty. I'm a bit worn out, so I pull the chair out and sit down comfortably in front of the monitors. For a few seconds, I just take the time to breathe and close my eyes.

Once I've recovered a bit, I lift my head to look at the main screen and the cams. On the *Skeld*, there are four security cameras and, in accordance with legal regulations, they are only pointed at transit areas, namely the hallways. And due to the same regulations, the cameras don't record any foot-age—they merely provide a live feed to Security. From my seat, I can very clearly see the hallway that separates the Upper Engine and the Cafeteria; a large part of the maze of the O2-Navigation-Weapons area; the intersection between the Cafeteria, Admin, and Storage; and, finally, the hallway that connects Security to the Reactor.

I try to pay close attention to this area since it lets me see if anyone is approaching the room I'm in. Even though I'm not doing anything wrong, I don't want to be caught spying. No need to attract unnecessary suspicion. Watching the cams carefully, I make detailed notes in my document of the slight-est details regarding the comings and goings of my crewmates.

Alice goes up to the Cafeteria, and then I find her between O2 and Navigation a few minutes later. Flavius goes down to MedBay, only stays there a few seconds, and then turns around. Livia is spending a lot of time in Storage. All in all, it's not anything unusual, but if you really think about it, any of these behaviors could appear suspicious.

I continue to make a note of the crew's movements for a good half hour until I see JC between the Cafeteria and the Upper Engine. On the monitor, I see him walk by quickly in his black spacesuit, then turn around and . . . start dancing.

Oh no! I had completely forgotten! The cameras flash when they're active. JC knows someone is watching. Others, too, if they were paying attention. I have to hurry. JC will surely get to Security any minute, and I don't want him to find me here. He also watches the cam feeds from time to time. But I don't want him to know that I'm doing it too.

I need to be able to play certain cards when I need them, without anyone knowing anything. I don't want the others to think I'm acting suspiciously.

I quickly shut off the monitors and rush out of the room. I glance down the hallway and don't see JC yet, but I hear his footsteps approaching. I almost run to the Lower Engine, then I turn left and go to Electrical. When I get there, I stand in front of the panel and pretend to tinker with some wires to catch my breath. Phew! That was close!

Once I've recovered, I close the document on my visor and reopen the list of tasks I still have to do. I still have work mostly at the other end of the ship in Shields and Navigation. As I set off again, a new alarm blares throughout the *Skeld*. On my visor, the words "REACTOR MELTDOWN" flash in red. That can't be right! What is it this time?

I walk toward the Reactor, trying to remember my training basics. This kind of meltdown is as rare as it is critical, and there's no time to waste. If I remember correctly, it takes two to repair the problem. Each person has to place their hand on a digital scanner in two different parts of the room. I hope that my crewmates are close by and that they won't expect someone else to do the dirty work for them while they quietly continue their tasks! In MIRA, there's this famous joke about a ship having exploded because none of the crew bothered to cancel the meltdown since they all thought their crewmates would take care of it. I never knew if this was true or just a story the instructors made up to teach us a lesson. I don't think I really want to know the answer to that today.

In the hallway leading to the Reactor, I see Livia coming out of the room. When she notices me, she turns around and goes back inside. I join her a few seconds later. I see Alice looking for the scanner and rush over to her side. I know exactly where it is. I waste no time and put my hand in the space provided for this purpose. Livia must be doing the same thing because after a few seconds, the alarm stops. We prevented the Reactor meltdown! When I turn around, Janelle is with Livia, and JC and Juihan have just come in.

Why did JC take so long to get here? I thought he was headed to Security. Maybe he took the time to look at who was doing what before deigning to join us?

"What the hell was that?" Livia asks breathlessly.

I'd like to answer her and ask her to explain her strange behavior when I arrived, but I don't have time. Flavius storms into the Reactor room.

"I'm always getting here when everything is over!" he jokes, shrugging. "But isn't it against the new rules to have so many people in such a small space?"

"Flavius is right," says JC. "Disperse!"

His bossy attitude is getting tiresome. I'd love to give him a piece of my mind, but I'm holding back. It wouldn't help to single myself out like that. While everyone returns to their tasks, I try to discreetly record what I saw. The way Livia was weirdly going back and forth; the fact that Alice was here; that JC arrived late when he was just next door; and Janelle, Juihan, and Flavius arriving late too. Does our survival matter so little to him? I also note that Doc was absent. While we all know that she has other things to do and that she has been temporarily relieved of her duties, I try to be as exhaustive as possible. Isn't the saying "the devil is in the details"? If that's true, then I'll be better prepared than anyone else to find it!

When I finish taking notes and leave the Reactor, the hallways are empty. I only see Flavius in Security, busy fixing wiring. To get to Shields, I go through the Lower Engine room and through Storage where JC and Janelle are busy with their tasks. Once at my destination, I sit in front of the monitor to prime the shields. When I tap on the screen, I hear a loud CLICK. What was that? A bit panicked, I hurry and finish my task so I can inspect the room. Everything looks normal . . . at least, that's what I think until I decide to keep going on my way.

That's when I realize that all the doors in the room have been locked. I rush over to one of them and try to manually unlock it. No luck. It doesn't budge. I bang wildly on the cold metal, screaming. Maybe someone will hear me and open it? But it's a waste of time: these doors are designed to be airtight to prevent all kinds of disasters. I'd be surprised if they let any sound through. I massage my temples and try to come up with a solution.

KLANG! KLANG! KLANG!

What the hell is that? I quickly turn away from the door, trying my best to identify the source of the noise.

KLANG! KLANG! KLANG!

It's resonating in my chest and my head so much that I can't tell whether the noise is coming closer or moving away. On the other hand, I now know where it's coming from. The air vents. What is making that noise?

KLANG! KLANG! KLANG!

The openings are way too small for anyone to fit through them . . . unless the virus somehow affects the physical properties of the person infected. Note to self: ask Doc about that, pending survival. My mouth feels dry, and I gulp loudly. For a moment, the noise in the vents stops.

I try to come to my senses. Why are these damn doors closed? How long am I going to stay locked up here?

Then, after an interminable minute, the noise resonates in the air vent again.

KLANG! KLANG! KLANG!

In a panic, I move as far away from it as possible, trying to hide as best I can. Whatever thing is lurking in there, I do not intend to be the first living being it encounters when it comes out.

After a minute or two, the noise subsides and then stops again. Cautiously, I come out of my hiding place. Maybe it was all in my head? Either Doc is right and aliens are roaming the vents, or I'm losing it. In the meantime, everything seems to have quieted. . . .

CLICK.

I can't suppress a jump. I quickly reassure myself that this is just the doors reopening. Phew!

I can finally get out of here! Slowly getting up, I smooth my spacesuit and check that I haven't inadvertently torn it. Everything looks okay. But my troubles aren't over. I haven't even left the room before a new alarm goes off. My visor displays "COMMUNICATIONS SABOTAGED."

I no longer have access to anything on my interface—my tasks, my document, everything has disappeared. What is going on? Is that what everything has been about since this morning? Sabotage?

I only have one thing I can do: go and reestablish comm systems as soon as possible. I have to get to Communications. I run out to the hallway . . . and immediately find myself facedown on the floor. My feet got caught on something, and I tripped.

I get up as best I can and turn around to see what I tripped over. I am in shock. I want to cry out in fear, but no sound comes out of my throat.

There is blood everywhere. On the body, on the walls, on the floor, on my spacesuit . . .

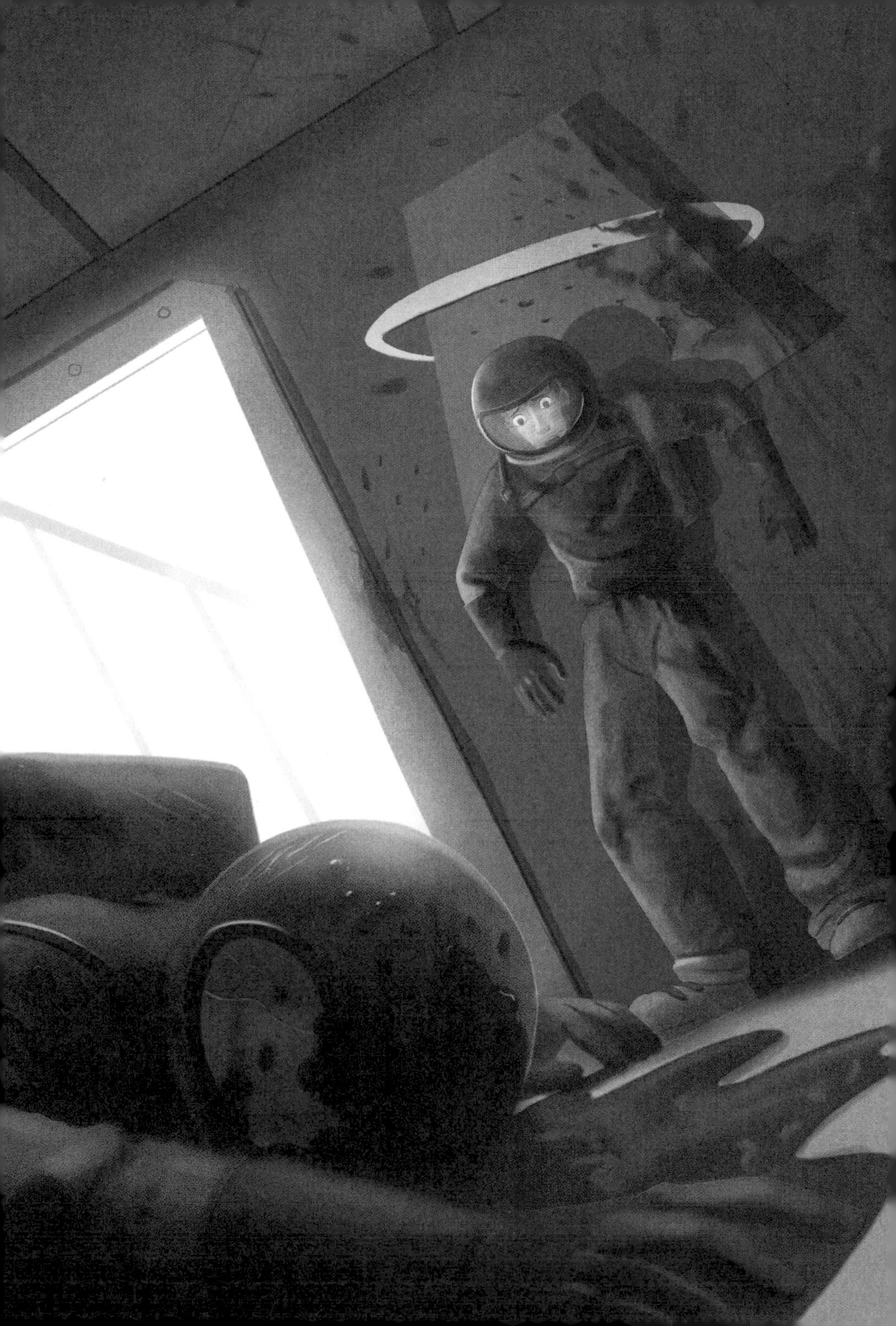

Instinctively, I look for the "Report" button on my visor. But the controls are all still blocked. I've got to make a decision quickly. The others will get to Communications soon and find me here, next to the body, my spacesuit covered in blood.

When I lift up my head and look around, I notice that the hallway is deserted. This is when it hits me: in my panic, I took the wrong exit. I am not at all near Communications, but in the hallway that leads to Navigation. What do I do next? Do I turn around to go and fix communications and risk someone seeing me leave the body all covered in blood? Or should I wait to report the body even if someone finds me standing there next to a corpse? No matter what choice I make, if anyone sees me, I'll look guilty.

I could run away, but if I see someone on the way, and the corpse is found where I came from, I'm done . . . I don't even have time to make a decision.

After a few seconds, communications are reestablished. Now I have to figure out if I report what's happened or run!

The doors locking when I was alone; the noise in the air vents; communications sabotaged, then repaired almost immediately; and the corpse just in front of the door, away from the cameras, outside the room I was just in . . . Someone is clearly trying to frame me.

And I need to figure out how to defend myself.

Chapter 12

In the Cafeteria, my crewmates begin to arrive. It didn't take long for me to make my decision: report the corpse.

While waiting for everyone to arrive, I try to collect myself. I feel like if I were to try to speak right now, the only thing that would come out of my mouth would be vomit. My stomach and brain seem to have switched places. Seriously, how do you go about telling everyone something like this? Like, "Yes, hello, sorry for disturbing you, but I just tripped over a dead body."

The few people who are already here are looking at me with wide eyes. I'd almost forgotten that my spacesuit is covered in blood. Judging by their expressions, I'm not the only one with my heart in my mouth. When there are seven of us in the room, I lift my head, straighten my back, and fix my gaze to a point in the distance above everyone.

"Are you going to tell us what happened?" Liv grows impatient.

"What's with all the blood on your spacesuit?" Flavius asks.

"Where's my mother?" Alice looks worried.

Alice. I had completely forgotten about her. When I saw Juihan's body, or at least what I think was Juihan, I didn't think of Alice. At all.

What was I going to say? Everything I had carefully pre-pared in the past few minutes is gone. All I can think of is how I felt when I learned my fathers were dead. It was cold and distant. A guy from MIRA had come to the house and spoken in lots of metaphors, as if I couldn't understand something so simple. My parents were dead. Why is it that not a single adult could summon the word? Dead.

Now, facing young Alice, I know. No one wants to be the one to tell a kid that they will never see their parents again. Everything I want to say to her gets stuck in my throat. I start to wonder if there are any right words for this.

She looks up at me with clear, wide eyes. "She's dead, too, right? Is that her blood on your spacesuit?"

My reply gets stuck in my mouth. I nod my head. "Yes," I managed to articulate. "I'm sorry."

The teen clenches her lips and teeth. Her cheeks and eyes go red. She doesn't say anything and doesn't cry. Still, I know her pain. I can feel it. Because I see her.

Janelle immediately walks up and puts her arms around Alice, hiding her face from me. Flavius, embarrassed but com-passionate, clumsily pats her shoulder. Behind them, Doc is looking grave and chewing on her lip.

"It means that the virus is still here," says Janelle, moving away from Alice. "And that . . . that maybe Henry was inno-cent." She grasps her helmet and plunges into silence.

All eyes converge on me, everyone waiting for me to speak.

"I found her body during the communications sabotage. I warned you as quickly as I could."

"Why do you have her blood all over you?" Livia asks suspiciously.

"When the comms alert went out, I rushed out of Shields. I didn't look where I was going and . . . well, I tripped."

"You stepped on her body?" JC asks, horrified.

"I, no, I slipped! There was blood everywhere; it was a mess. . . ." Thinking about Alice, I stop there and leave out the sordid details. She doesn't need that.

"And where was that?" Flavius asks.

"Right outside Shields. In the hallway to Navigation."

"What were you doing there while there was a communications sabotage going on?"

This is exactly what I was afraid of. And, of course, Livia is pouncing on it. "In all the chaos, I took the wrong door. . . ."

"Well, okay then. How convenient!" says Livia.

"What do you mean?" I ask her.

"You find the body *just* outside the room you locked yourself in for a few minutes, and outside of a door you had no reason to use!"

"I didn't lock myself in! I was locked in! There's a dif-fer-ence!"

"And who locked you in? These doors can't be locked remotely!"

"By the person who sabotaged communications! Isn't it obvious?"

Livia sighs and brushes off my argument with the back of her hand.

"What's your theory?" JC asks me.

"I think that someone deliberately locked me in Shields long enough to commit this crime. The communications sabotage then prevented me from reporting the body and left me in an awkward position where I would have been seen coming out of a room near where the body would have been found later. It's ingenious, really. Unfortunately for the person who did this, my terrible sense of direction messed up their plans."

"That's quite the story," says Flavius.

"Or," Livia begins, "*you* closed the doors to Shields to perpetrate *your* crime, and *you* sabotaged communications to have time to escape without anyone being able to report the body during this time. Unfortunately for you, I was near Communications, and I was able to fix the problem very quickly."

"You were the one who fixed the comms?" I ask.

"Yeah. Alice can confirm it. She arrived a little after me and saw me doing it."

"How did you manage to get there so quickly? The sabotage only lasted a few seconds."

"I was going there for a task."

"Oh, how convenient."

"What are you implying?"

"Nothing at all . . . Only, how did you know that the Shields doors were locked? I hadn't shared that yet."

"Because I got stuck on the other side of the door!"

"What were you doing there?"

"I was going from Navigation to Storage. I had to take a detour when I found out the door was locked."

"Or maybe you're the one who locked them! And you sabotaged comms for only a few seconds as soon as the doors reopened, knowing that I would just have been leaving the room near where the corpse would be found."

"Why would I have sabotaged the comms just to un-sabotage them? Come on, don't be ridiculous, V!"

"Seriously! If it were me, do you really think I would have brought you all here with the victim's blood all over my spacesuit? It just doesn't make sense!"

"You might be stupid, I don't know."

"Smart enough to come up with the Machiavellian plan you're describing, but not smart enough to avoid detection? So which is it? Be consistent!"

"Stop it! Stop it!" JC's voice echoes throughout the Cafeteria. "Let's start again. Calmly this time, okay? The evidence points to at least one of us being infected by that damn virus. We'll have to think about what happens next. If we make the decision to eject someone who is *not* infected, we all put ourselves in more danger in the future. I suggest that everyone skip the vote."

"Excuse me?" Liv takes offense. "Someone *here* has committed two murders, and you're saying we should just let them get away with it?"

"And I thought you were on the let's-find-a-cure-and-not-kill-anyone team," I respond.

"Well, things have changed again, haven't they?"

"Oh, really?"

"Well, I don't want to die. So if we have to sacrifice the infected person to make it out of this, that's fine by me."

"You mean me?"

"Maybe."

"Remember how well that worked the last time you denounced someone?"

"That's cruel, V."

"He's right though," says Flavius. "You keep changing your mind. It's not very consistent."

"Who asked you? We don't even know what the hell you did today. You're always the last one to show up when something goes wrong, and the rest of the time you wander around the hallways with half of your tasks incomplete."

"Oh, so I'm the target now. I'm not the best crewmate, sure, but that shouldn't make me a suspect. I have faults. I'm a slacker, but I'm no murderer!" Flavius yells.

"Liv, you can't just start accusing everyone again to exonerate yourself!" JC says.

"And why not? If you think about it, you've all been acting suspiciously! Especially you!" she retorts.

"Oh, have I?"

"You have! You spend your life in Security watching cams, and when the reactor melts down *right next door,* you're not even the first in the room to fix it."

"Well, now I've heard everything. . . ." JC exhales.

"But don't worry, you're not the only one. You've also got to wonder what Doc is up to. After all, no one knows since she spends all night and day in MedBay."

Doc looks like she's about to respond, but Liv doesn't even give her time.

"We could also ask Alice to explain to us why she was still there during the meltdown."

"Livia!" Flavius yells. "Are you serious? After everything that's happened? Going after Alice?"

"I don't really believe it, Flavius. I'm just pointing out everyone's strange behavior."

"What about Janelle?" I ask.

"I trust her," Livia says.

"Lucky her," I say. "What about you?"

"What about me?" Livia snaps.

"Are we going to talk about your questionable behavior?"

"What behavior is that?"

"When the Reactor was melting down, I saw you leaving the room. When you saw me, you quickly turned around to go back in. Why?"

"I came out when I saw that there was no one in there. It takes two people to stop the meltdown. I was going to find someone."

"That's not true! Alice was there."

"But . . . I . . . I didn't see her. I swear."

"You were also the first to arrive to fix the sabotage in Communications!"

"That's just a coincidence."

"And what about the fact that Janelle has thought you've been acting strange the past few days. Is that a coincidence too?"

"Wait, what?"

Livia looks back and forth between me and her girlfriend. She looks panicked. Janelle seems to be back with us. Tears are pouring from her eyes. She turns to me and looks at me in disbelief.

I hadn't thought before opening my mouth. Janelle confided in me because she trusted me, and I just betrayed her by throwing everything at Livia to unsettle her. In front of everyone.

"Janelle, what's he saying?" Livia asks.

Janelle can't even answer her.

"Janelle, what the hell is he talking about?" Livia is getting angry, rushing toward her girlfriend.

When Livia grabs her by the arm, Janelle finally reacts. "It's true, Liv. I confided in V because for the past few days, I haven't recognized you anymore. Just like this!" she says, pulling her arm free of Livia's grasp.

"So you think I'm guilty too?" Livia asks wearily.

"I don't know, Liv. I'm not sure. I don't know what to think anymore."

This is when the countdown to the vote begins. In just a few seconds, we will all have to make a choice.

Livia remains silent, looking at Janelle, seeming to search for the answer to all her questions.

I turn to Doc. Her eyes are on me. I understand from her expression that she is determined not to reveal anything of her discoveries. I decide to do the same. Keeping this secret could be useful to us, and together we could tip the scales if we have to vote. Like now. Like next time.

"So what do we do?" Flavius asks.

All eyes converge on Livia, who is sinking into a dark rage.

"So that's it? The die is cast? I'm the one you're blaming? Janelle, why the hell did you talk to that asshole? Can't you see he's using what you said to destroy me? You can't trust him!"

As she unleashes her anger, Livia moves dangerously close to Janelle. Flavius steps in between the two, to keep Livia from turning violent, but that only seems to make her angrier. Her screams echo throughout the Cafeteria, her voice broken and disjointed. She's choking, crying, and it makes her impossible to understand.

The countdown continues.

5, 4, 3, 2, 1 . . .

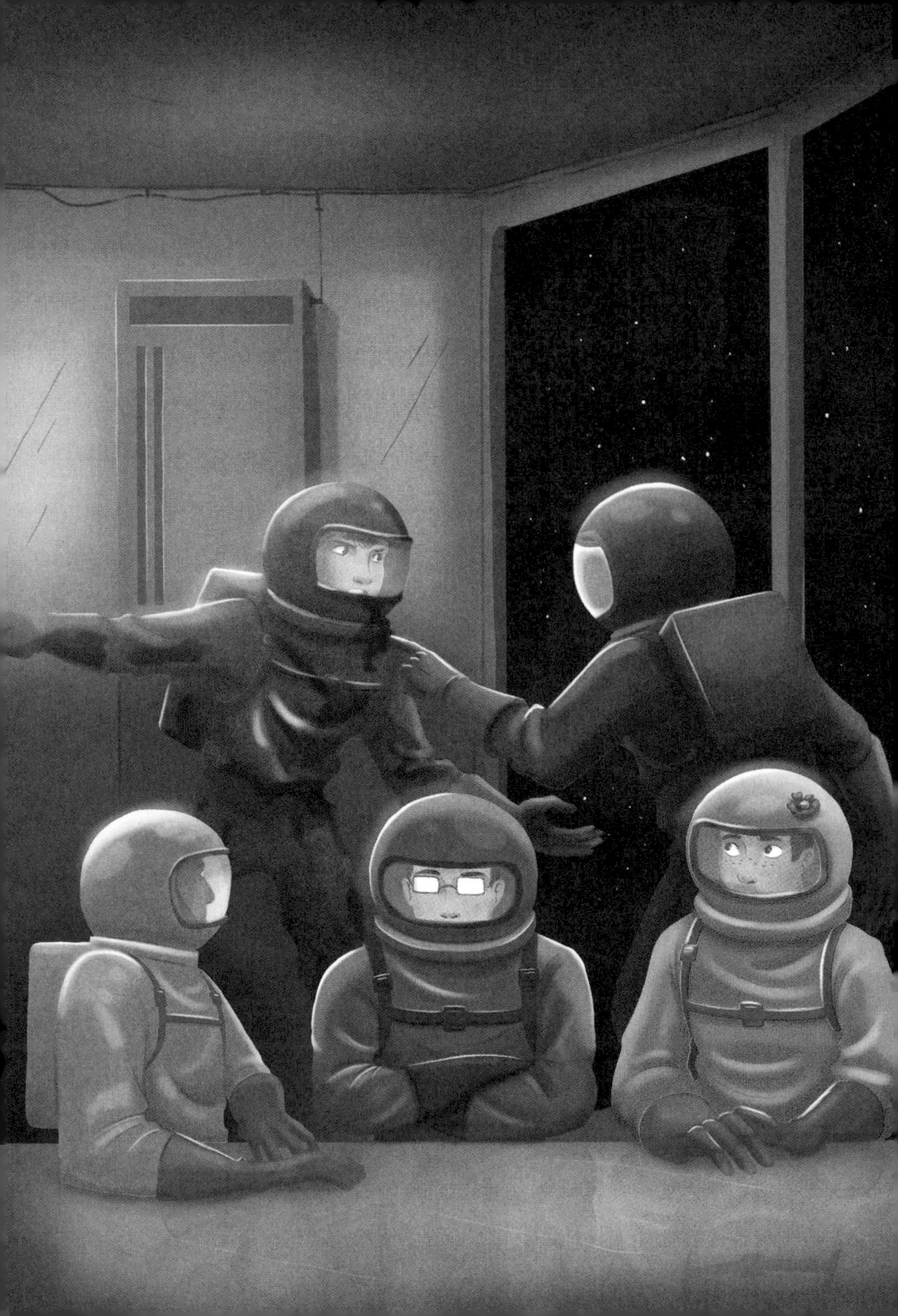

Chapter 13

CALCULATING RESULTS.

The votes are displayed one after the other on our visors.

And the result is in: six votes against Livia, one against me. So Janelle must have voted against her girlfriend.

I can see the moment when Livia realizes this, the rage distorting her face. She throws herself at Janelle but is stopped by Flavius and JC. She screams and struggles as if possessed. They have to work together to control her.

She directs her anger at Janelle first, throwing insults at her. "Why? Why did you do that? How could you? Janelle! Explain yourself! Who made you change your mind? Tell me! Janelle, damn it, Janelle, talk to me! I never would have done that to you! I thought we trusted each other. You've betrayed me!"

Janelle looks scared. She gasps and cries, like she's unable to respond.

Then Livia changes her tone. "I'm so sorry, babe, I'm sorry. I know it's not your fault. I know you didn't want this. I forgive you, Janelle. They all used you. They got you all worked up. I understand. But I'm innocent, I promise. Baby, look at me, please. Please."

Janelle doesn't look up. It's like she can't. She just stays there, frozen, a few yards from Livia, unable to move or speak.

Then Livia's rage takes over again. "It's him, right? It's that asshole who put you up to this? V, you're dead. I'm gonna kill you."

She focuses on me now, accusing me of manipulating Janelle to get her vote. She screams that the infected, the impostor, is me. That I'm lying to everyone, that I'm collecting secrets that I'll use to stab them all in the back as soon as I have the opportunity.

She then turns to everyone else and tells them she's seen me taking notes all day. "What for, V? Was that where you wrote down all your plans? Show us, if you dare! Show us everything you've written! Who's going to be next after me? Huh? Tell us, V! We're all listening!"

I pretend I have no idea what she's talking about and shrug. Even though I have nothing to hide, I don't want to let others think there is a shred of truth in Livia's accusations. I don't answer and let the storm pass.

Judging by their expressions, my crewmates don't seem to believe what Livia is saying. Somehow, we are all trying to convince ourselves that she's really guilty—well, infected—and that we've made the right decision. The only possible decision.

When Livia doesn't get a reaction from me, she goes after someone else. Flavius, who has been struggling to control her for a few minutes, is the next target of her wrath. "And you, new guy! Do you think I haven't noticed all your crap? I know you have a crush on my girlfriend. Is that why you want to kill me? You want her all to yourself, huh? That's never going to work, buddy. She's never going to want you."

Livia raises the visor of her helmet and spits on Flavius's helmet. He recoils and lets go of her. She then manages to get out of JC's grasp and throws herself at Janelle's feet.

"Janelle, I'm innocent, I swear. . . ."

Flavius wipes off his helmet. Then he and JC restrain her again.

"Come on, this has gone on long enough," JC says before pushing her forward.

The two of them somehow manage to drag Livia out of the Cafeteria.

Her screams get twice as loud, but her sentences no longer make any sense. Janelle rushes after them. I am about to do the same, then I think of Alice. I turn toward her. I don't want to leave her alone.

Doc signals for me to leave, that she'll stay with Alice and wait for us to get back. So I run down the hallway leading to the escape hatch.

I quickly catch up to Janelle, who is shaking and crying. Putting an arm around her shoulders, I try to figure out what to say to her.

She is the first to speak. "Oh, V, do you think we were wrong? What did I do?" she asks, looking up at me with swollen, red eyes.

"All the evidence pointed to her," I whisper.

I don't know who I'm trying to convince, me or her. Livia's many strange behaviors, her temper tantrums, and her way of accusing anyone when she felt cornered all suggest that Livia isn't innocent. But still, there is always a chance. In the absence of irrefutable proof, or an eyewitness, we can't be sure of anything. Obviously, I keep my doubts to myself and don't say a word to Janelle. Instead, I try to reassure her, reminding her that she thought Livia was acting weird, that we voted unanimously, and that if it wasn't her, who would it be? Janelle seems to calm down a bit. She's stopped crying and bombarding me with questions, at least. She walks ahead with her back straight, her eyes locked on the three crewmates struggling to move forward in front of us. Livia hasn't stopped screaming.

When we get to the airlock, JC asks me to unlock it and configure the depressurization and the outer door opening. I start by lifting the handle to open the airlock. JC and Flavius are struggling to bring Livia in, and Livia is now begging for our forgiveness.

"You're making a mistake, guys. . . . Please . . . listen to me, damn it. It's not me, I swear! This is ridiculous! Please, I'm sorry. . . . I'm sorry, let me go, let me explain. Don't do this!" She chokes on her sobs.

When Flavius pushes her aggressively to the other end of the small airlock, I lift the door handle. In an instant, the door separating her and us closes.

On the other side of the glass, Livia's voice sounds more distant. But the sound of her fists on the glass and her pleas are loud and clear. "Please! I'm begging you! I don't want to die! Janelle! Please . . . I'm scared! V, you can't let this happen! It's unfair—it's barbaric! You know it!"

I look away, trying to hide my face from the others, unable to face her. As I type on the interface to start depressurization, I start to wonder if she might be telling the truth. The countdown begins and drowns out Livia's words, which now sound choppy and indistinct.

Taking advantage of the commotion, Janelle rushes to the manual control. With one swift move, she lowers the handle. The countdown stops instantly, and the airlock door opens.

Livia, who clearly understands what is going on before we do, immediately tries to escape. JC is the first of the three of us to react, and he moves to block her. Janelle tries to push him, then trips over his leg and falls into the airlock. Her girlfriend turns around and looks at her before trying to escape again.

JC stands there, solid as a rock, and doesn't give her a chance. He shoves her back inside the airlock and throws himself on the handle. The door closes immediately, and the countdown picks up where it left off.

"What the hell are you doing, JC?" Flavius yells. "Janelle is inside!"

"We can't allow her to escape!"

"But Janelle is innocent!"

JC doesn't answer, but his face says it all. He won't budge, and if Flavius wants to save Janelle, he'll have to get past him. The two of them start fighting, and I approach the porthole. I put my face and hand to the glass, hypnotized. I'm helpless. I can't take my eyes off the two women on the other side, screaming and pleading. Next to me, JC and Flavius are fighting in front of the interface, each one trying to prevent the other from accessing the controls. In my head, all the noises blend together: the screams, the countdown, the sound of their fists, and the intermittent *BEEPS* of the keys they press. Then everything stops. The clock stops. Flavius and JC both look at the control panel, shocked. I force myself to look as well. The display shows: "DEPRESSURIZATION PROCEDURE COMPLETED." Then: "EXTERIOR DOOR RELEASE IMMINENT."

I then come to my senses and take advantage of a stunned Flavius and JC to try to open the door. I have to save Janelle! I try to operate the controls, to push the buttons, and that's when it dawns on me: while fighting, JC and Flavius broke the controls. Nothing's responding anymore. We can't cancel this, even manually.

"What have you done?!" I yell.

Livia and Janelle must understand something's happening because I can't hear them anymore. I bring my fist down in anger on the broken controls. Hot tears roll down my cheeks.

Suddenly, a new countdown breaks the silence. This one is different, its tone strangely sweet. How ironic. *DOOR OPENING IN 20, 19, 18 . . .*

In a last desperate attempt, I rush to the airlock door. I grab the handles and try to pull them open. Of course, that won't work. I know it. Janelle and Livia know it. Everyone knows it. When the countdown reaches five, I face the facts and give up. I look up and through the porthole. Tears and rage cloud my vision, yet I can see it distinctly: Janelle and Livia have stopped struggling. They hug each other in a last embrace, one that will be frozen for eternity.

   . . . 3, 2, 1 . . .

A beep sounds. The door at the end of the airlock opens, and space sucks out the two lovers in a fraction of a second.

My anguished scream echoes throughout the ship.

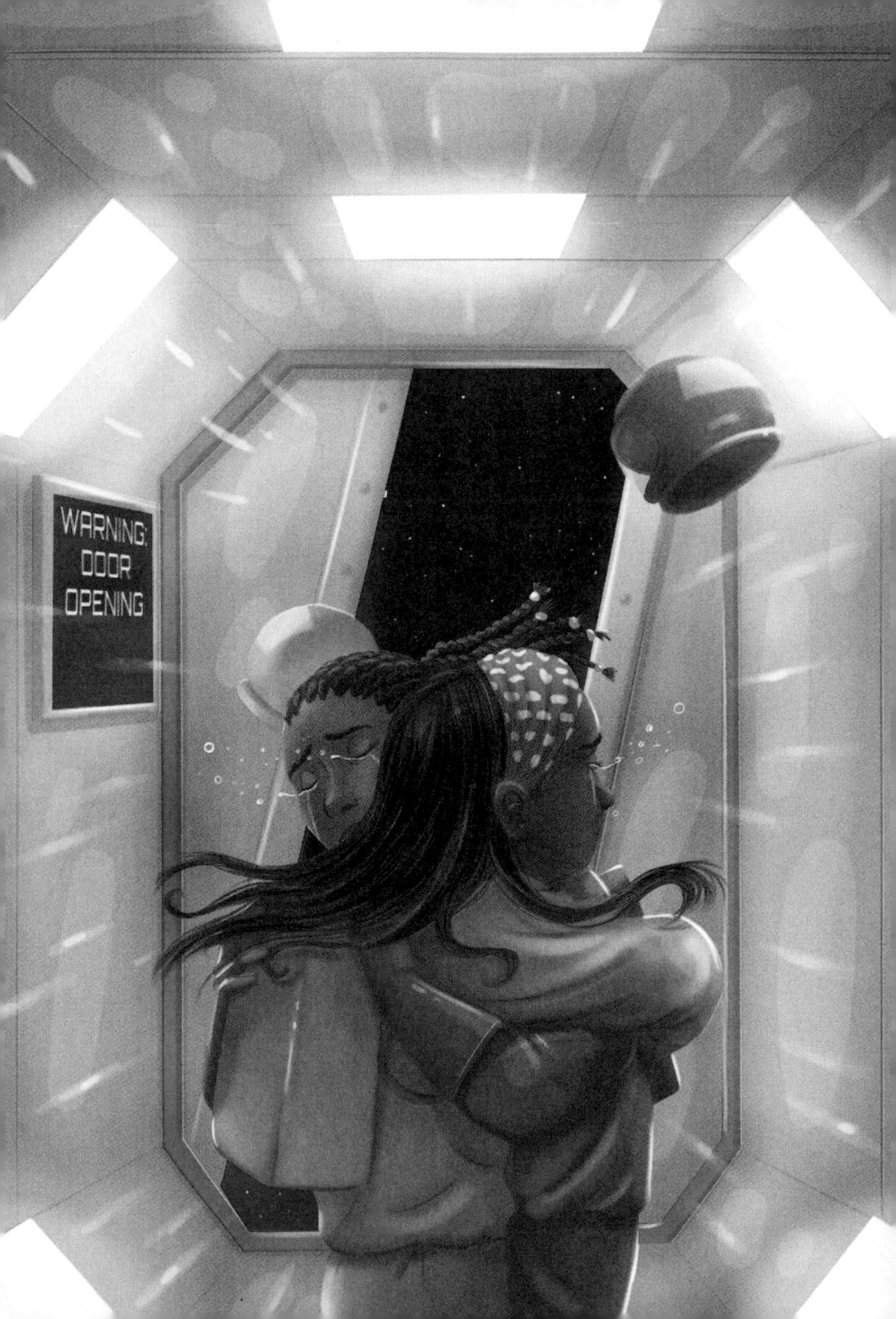
WARNING:
DOOR
OPENING

It only takes a few seconds for the outer door to close. And another few for the airlock pressure to return to normal. All the mechanisms have stopped, and the silence is deafening. I can feel my legs giving out, but I don't fall. I stay there, incredibly still, leaning against the porthole. Just like the rest of the ship, I'm frozen in disbelief. Was that real? Or was it a nightmare? If I turn around, will Janelle be there, giving me one of those I've-got-a-secret smiles? Deep down, I know that's not going to happen. Janelle and Livia are dead. And there was nothing I could do about it.

After their short truce, JC and Flavius start fighting again. It brings me back to the present. Flavius is hurling insults at JC while trying to hit him. JC is trying his best to ward off all the blows.

"I had to! It was the only thing to do . . . the only solution," he yells between blows.

I hear footsteps in the hallway, and soon Doc and Alice appear. Doc steps in to separate the two fighting men.

"What is happening here? We heard you screaming from the Cafeteria!" she yells, holding each one by the neck.

"That bastard killed Janelle and Liv!" yells Flavius.

"What? What are you talking about?"

"I had no choice!" JC insists.

Before JC and Flavius go at it again, Doc tells them to quit it and tell her what happened.

They talk over one another at first; then, finally, Flavius lets JC tell the story.

"Janelle lost it," explains JC. "She interrupted the whole thing in an attempt to save Livia. I did what I could to keep Liv from escaping. Doc, you should have seen her eyes! Bloodshot! I felt like she would have killed me without a second thought if it gave her any kind of advantage. In the chaos, Janelle tripped and ended up in the airlock. I wanted to help her, but I couldn't risk Livia escaping. As soon as I was able to control her, I pushed her back into the airlock and closed the door. I wanted to think of a way to get Janelle out of there, I swear, except Flavius attacked me. While we were fighting, we broke the controls. Then there was no going back. There was nothing more we could do, Doc—it was too late."

"You mean that . . . ?"

"Livia and Janelle were ejected," Flavius says, his fists clenched.

Doc stares at JC. I wonder what she's thinking. Is his explanation credible? Does he really regret what happened? Or is Janelle's death just collateral damage to him? These are the questions I've been asking myself the past few minutes.

I don't think the answer really matters though. The facts are there, immutable. I lost one of my best friends on this ship because of this guy. So his excuses and remorse—he can shove them.

Flavius, taking advantage of Doc's momentary distraction, attacks JC again. He goes after him with everything he's got.

Doc lets out a long sigh before intervening again. Once she has the two separated, she says, "That's enough, you two! What is done is done, and we'll come back to it in due course. For now, there are other priorities, so you will both listen to me, is that clear?"

Like kids caught red-handed, JC and Flavius nod their heads, their eyes downcast.

"Good. JC, you come with me," she orders him. "We're going to collect Juihan's body and bring her to MedBay. This will allow me to make progress in understanding this . . . this virus. Flavius, V, you two walk Alice to her sleeping pod. We've talked about it: she's relieved of all duties until further notice. The regulations are very clear about minors working when parents or caregivers are . . . absent."

Flavius and JC signal their approval.

Doc turns to me. "V? Did you hear me? . . . V? Are you okay?"

The gentleness in her voice brings me abruptly back to reality. "Yes. Alice. To her pod. With Flavius." These are the only words I can get out.

Doc stares at me for a few more moments, then decides to take JC with her before he and Flavius start fighting again.

"Should we go?" asks Flavius.

I nod.

"Are you coming, Alice?" he adds.

He's talking to her like a baby. Or a dog, I don't know. Alice, however, doesn't seem bothered by it and follows him. I roll my eyes. This guy is ridiculous. It makes you wonder how he's managed to survive when half the crew has been wiped out.

Half. Already. Thinking of this sends a shiver down my spine. How much longer before it's my turn?

I finally come out of my gruesome thoughts when Flavius grabs my shoulder.

"Hey, don't you think JC was acting strange?" he whispers so that Alice, who is up ahead, doesn't hear.

At first, I don't answer.

That doesn't stop my crewmate. "His account doesn't make sense. He never wanted to help Janelle, I swear. I mean, you saw it too. He didn't even consider her. He only wanted to make sure Livia didn't escape. But what if . . ." He pauses, no doubt convinced that he's a great master of suspense.

"What if what?" I say so he finally gets to the point.

"I was thinking. What if—I wasn't paying close attention— what if he tripped Janelle. *On purpose*, to make her fall into the airlock."

"Why would he do that?"

"Who knows! Maybe to create a diversion and to better control Livia. Or maybe because he just wanted to kill someone else! There could be so many reasons!"

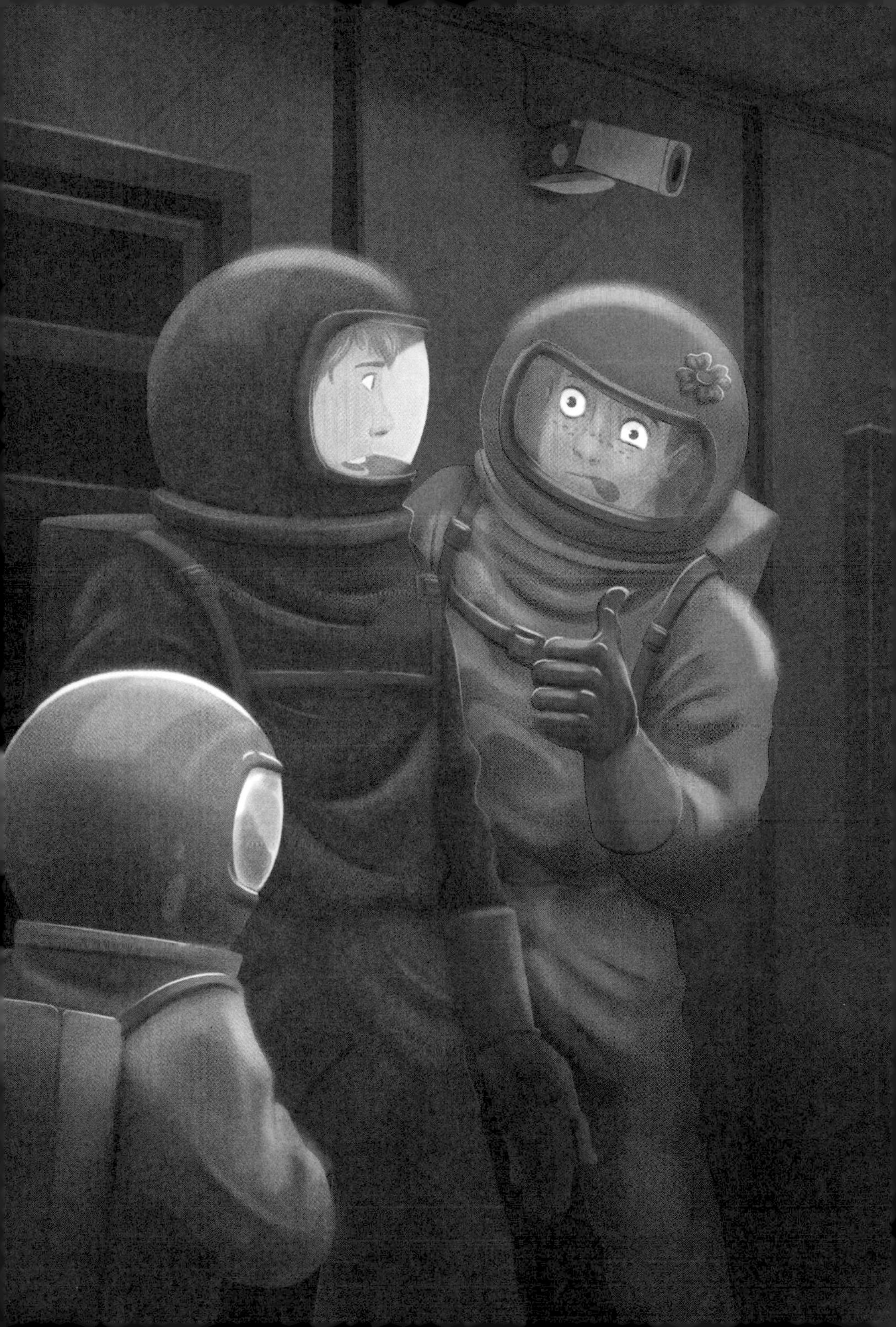

I stop in the middle of the hallway. "What are you trying to say, Flavius?"

"There's something not quite right about this guy. That's all. He's always playing mister know-it-all, mister boss man. It's weird, isn't it?"

"Do you think he's the impostor?"

"I don't have any proof, of course, but after what we just saw, I have my suspicions. Don't you?"

"I don't know. I am so confused. I was convinced it was Livia. Well, I think so."

"I hope that we were right and that we made the right choice too," says Flavius. "But if we got it wrong, I'd rather play it safe. I'm telling you about it because you seem like a good guy. Janelle's death really hurt you, I can tell. And I don't think an infected person could react like that, do you?"

I shrug.

"All this to say, watch out for JC. If I were you, I would avoid being alone with him, because . . ." He runs his thumb across his throat.

We finally arrive at Alice's pod. She thanks us and gives us a brief wave before entering. When the door closes behind her, I tell Flavius that I will return to my tasks. We are all far behind.

"Yeah, you're right." He nods. "But think about what I said . . . and watch out for *him,* okay?"

"Okay."

"And if you see him doing anything fishy, like really fishy, you tell me, all right?"

"If you want, sure."

He sighs. "V, we have to stay united. There are only five of us left."

He's about to pat me on the shoulder, but I pull away abruptly.

"Okay, I get it," he says. "You don't trust me?"

"It's not you," I argue. "I'm suspicious of everyone, that's all."

"Oh? Even Alice?" He pauses. "Even Doc?"

I don't answer.

"I see I'm on your shit list. That's too bad. I guess I'm going to be all alone. Whatever. I'm used to it." He spins on his heels and leaves me without looking back.

All alone in the hallway, I try to force myself to get back to work. But I can't. My body no longer obeys me. I feel like I'm just a shell, emptied of all vital energy, of all feeling. I switch to autopilot. My legs move under me, and I automatically head to complete the tasks I have left. I feel like I've become a robot, heartless, soulless, whose only goal is to work on this ship for eternity. It keeps me from thinking. And from feeling, most of all. I have to do what I can to avoid thinking about Janelle, about what happened.

Or what could happen . . .

Chapter 15

The next day, I wake up feeling slow and groggy, like I'd slept for days even though I'd only slept for a few hours—and poorly at that. I couldn't get the images out of my head: Janelle and Livia being ejected. Then I went over and over everything I did and everything I could have done differently. It didn't do much beyond making me feel even more guilty. Now, I'm groggy and tired, and I haven't even started my day yet. I have to force myself to get out of my pod. Once in the hallway, I decide to skip breakfast. I'm not hungry anyway.

I might as well get work over with as soon as possible. I'll then have plenty of time to wander the ship aimlessly, alone in my thoughts. Like a ghost.

I switch myself on autopilot again. I go to Weapons and clear asteroids without really paying attention. I upload data in Admin without really thinking about it. I slide, slide, and slide my damn card through the reader without showing any outward sign of annoyance. I empty the Cafeteria garbage almost without realizing it.

As I drag my feet in the hallway between the Cafeteria and the Upper Engine, I hear someone behind me.

"Hey, V!"

I turn around. No one's in the hallway.

"On your right!"

I turn to MedBay. Doc's helmet is barely protruding from the doorway.

"What's going on?" I ask sluggishly.

"I have to show you something. Get in here, quickly, before JC sees you on cams."

I take a look at the cameras. They are switched off right now. Without quite knowing why, I follow Doc inside. She pulls aside the plastic tarp and lets me enter her lair. The space has been split in two. On one side there's a big table piled high with computer and medical equipment. On the other side there's a second plastic tarp, a very stained one, leading to what must be her real lab. I don't even want to know what's back there.

Doc grabs a large spray bottle from the table and brings it over to me.

"What is that?" I pull away, worried.

"Disinfectant. For your spacesuit."

"What for?"

Without a word, she points her chin to the other side of the room.

"Can't you just . . . explain?"

"It's better to show you."

"I'm not sure I'm ready for that."

"V, this is not the time."

I gulp loudly. "Okay."

Doc sprays my whole spacesuit with a hydroalcoholic spray. She then puts the bottle back down behind her and spreads apart two tarps.

"After you." She mimics a curtsy.

I imagined a lot of things. But what I see on the stretchers is worse than all of them. Instinctively, I close my eyes and take a step back. Doc is behind me, preventing me from running away.

"Take your time if you need to," she whispers, going around me.

I inhale slowly and open my eyes again. There are two human bodies in front of me. It looks like Doc has taken them apart and put them back together again. I try to keep myself from retching.

"Was this really necessary?" I finally manage to ask.

"It will be easier to understand if you can see it—easier for you to believe it too."

"I have a very good imagination, you know. And I trust you. . . ."

She brushes aside my arguments. "Listen, V, this is *really* important. But if you don't feel like you can handle it, it's okay—you can go. I thought you'd be interested, but maybe I was wrong."

Doc is right. I have to get over myself. She wouldn't have dragged me here if she didn't have something crucial to tell me.

"What is it?"

I try to give her a smile, and she returns one to me immediately. Her eyes sparkle as she gets ready to tell me what she's unearthed. It would be endearing if it weren't for the two wide-open corpses in front of us.

"I'd already had some theories—well, general ideas, really—when I was studying Raymond's body. But I didn't have enough data to confirm anything. I was just guessing. But getting to study Juihan's body allowed me to refute some things—and to confirm others. Come closer and take a look."

I don't really want to, but I don't think I have a choice. I clench my jaw and approach the stretcher with Juihan's remains.

When I found her body, the hallway hadn't been very well lit. I remember her body there, bisected, covered in blood, with blood on the walls. And it'd looked like her intestines were slowly leaving her body like crawling insects. I'll admit that I didn't look much closer at the time. The green of her blood-covered spacesuit was enough information for me: the identity of body. I hadn't thought all that much more about . . . the rest.

Now that Juihan is lying in front of me without her spacesuit on, I realize the extent of the damage. And it's not particularly pleasant to look at. From her head to her feet, there are lots of places where her skin is torn open, like a million small knife cuts. The gashes are so large in places that you can see blood, bone, other strange viscous fluids, and stuff

I can't identify. How is this possible? What could have gone through her spacesuit like that?

In front of me, Doc is watching my face and looking excited. She's giving me time to ask myself questions and develop my own theories. I know none of them will live up to what she is about to tell me.

"So, what do you think?" Doc asks me, clearly fighting back a smile.

"This is disgusting."

"I mean, isn't there something that you find shocking?"

"Pretty much everything."

Doc rolls her eyes and shrugs. She turns around and rummages through a cabinet. When she turns back around, she's holding out Juihan's spacesuit. Or half of it.

"And now?" she asks me.

"Hmm . . . it's cut in half and covered in blood."

"And?"

"Um . . ."

"Are you really that unobservant, V? Look at the gashes on Juihan's arms, then look at the sleeves of her spacesuit."

I do what she asks. Juihan's arms, like her chest and legs, are torn all over the place. Then I look at the spacesuit Doc is holding out. There are no lacerations.

"Oh," I whisper.

"You see it now?"

"The wounds . . . her skin . . . she . . . well, that . . ."

"The cuts were caused by something internal, not external."

127

"Yeah. That . . . but how is that even possible?"

"It's our alien!" she announces proudly. "I was right! The alien life-form tries to infect our organs in order to grow, take control, and thrive. Its cellular activity is incredible, V! It's able to adapt to its host to permeate it and make it do its bidding . . . well, when the infection works, because apparently it's not completely successful yet."

I give her a bewildered look.

"Well, let me show you; it will make more sense."

At these words, she grabs a scalpel and pliers and goes for Juihan's gaping abdomen. With the scalpel, she lifts a flap of skin to reveal a mass of bloodred flesh and guts. At that point, I'm grateful I didn't have breakfast. I push myself to keep watching. With her other hand, Doc draws my attention to something that doesn't look like the intestines. It's a growth that looks like a tiny tentacle.

"What is that?" I gasp.

"The alien, trying to settle in."

"Oh."

"But for some reason I can't figure out, this doesn't always go well. The alien life-form begins to develop, but something goes wrong and it ends up killing its host . . . and itself too."

"How is that possible?"

"I don't know yet. It could be genetics, blood type, or something else? It's hard to say right now. Especially without being able to study the process working on someone."

I look down at the corpse in front of me. A little farther away, behind Doc, there's Raymond's body under a white sheet. What prompted the alien to infect these two people? Did they just end up in the wrong place at the wrong time? Or were these planned attacks? As I look from one to the other, something hits me.

"Could the alien have intentionally targeted the Stark-Lius?"

"That's a promising hypothesis, yes."

"Let's say it did. Why them?"

"A question of genetic diversity, perhaps. After failing to work on Raymond, it is possible that the alien sought out someone with a sufficiently different genetic heritage to optimize its chances. Again, that's only a guess . . ."

I cut her off. "Do you think Alice could be in danger?"

"I've asked myself the same thing. It's hard to say. . . . If my theory is correct, I'd say she's not. Her genetic heritage is a combination of Raymond's and Juihan's, so it's likely that the alien will look somewhere else first. Then, if there's still an alien presence on this ship . . . I believe that, with how few of us there are left, we're all in danger. The alien will fight to survive no matter what. Ultimately, we are all at risk of becoming infected."

I gulp loudly. Since yesterday, I've been trying to convince myself that Liv was the infected one and that the problem is now behind us. But there is still a chance that Liv was sane. Or that she had time to infect someone else before she was ejected. If that damn alien is still on the *Skeld*, then there's not much time left until each of us is cut in half or transformed into a native Polusian. Frankly, I don't know which of the two outcomes scares me more—dying or becoming an alien host. At that point, I think suicide might be an option.

"Doc, if this . . . life-form is still with us, we're all dead. Wouldn't it be better to blow up the ship right now, to eliminate the threat once and for all? What if we bring this thing back to Polus! It could be the end of humanity!"

My suggestion is an extreme one, and of course I don't like the idea, but do we really have another choice? How could we put so many people in danger just to live a few more hours or days?

To my surprise, Doc laughs.

"I'm serious, Doc. We have a real ethical responsibility here."

"I know, V, and it's honorable that you're willing to sacrifice yourself. . . . But I have a slightly less definitive alternative."

I widen my eyes. "What's that?"

"Well, I might have developed some kind of test capable of detecting the presence of aliens in our bodies."

I stay silent for a few seconds, dumbfounded.

"And you're only telling me this now?"

Chapter 16

"It's still more or less a prototype," Doc says.

"How effective is it?"

"If I didn't mess up my calculations, I would say, 95 percent but . . ."

"But nothing, Doc! This is exactly what we need! We test everyone, we get rid of the ones with a positive result, and that's that."

"It's not that simple," she says.

I don't get it. She's developed a reliable test that could definitely get us out of this mess, and she's finding a way to put it off?

"It seems very simple to me," I say. "Isn't that what we've wanted since this whole thing started? If your test works, then we don't have to agonize over thousands of tiny things. We just do it!"

Doc looks down thoughtfully. I walk around the stretcher with Juihan on it and grab Doc by the shoulders. She looks up at me.

"What's the matter, Doc?"

She takes a deep breath. "For you, 5 percent might not seem like much . . . but it's really huge. You said it yourself, V: we have an ethical responsibility. And there's an even bigger problem. Ninety-five percent reliability means we risk having false negatives. Or false positives. Do you get what that means?"

I get it. Between sparing the real impostor or condemning an innocent person, the slightest mistake could cost us dearly. For my part, I'm convinced that it's a risk we have to take.

"But, Doc," I yell, "it's much more accurate than our impulsive pseudo-court system!"

Doc seems to consider my argument for an instant, but then she pulls back. "We need to think about this at least! It's not the kind of decision we can take lightly!"

"Who said I wanted to take it lightly?" I reply.

"Just listen to yourself. It only took you a matter of seconds to decide."

"Because I've been thinking about all this for days! And it's all gotten even worse since yesterday afternoon. . . . I have played out every scenario in my head. A reliable test, even an almost reliable test—that was more of a dream than a possible scenario. So yes, I do think it's worth the chance."

Doc doesn't look convinced. Her eyes flutter, and I guess she's going over everything I've said in her mind. I can tell that she wants to argue with me, but we're interrupted by a noise.

"What is that?" I whisper, panicked.

With a furrowed brow and her index finger pressed against her visor, Doc tells me to be quiet.

The noise quickly becomes recognizable. Someone has just entered MedBay and has approached the tarps of Doc's makeshift lab.

"Doc? Is everything all right?"

It's JC. Damn it, this guy is such a stalker. He's always following me around.

Doc doesn't panic. She signals that I shouldn't speak or move. I don't object.

"Yes. Is there a problem?" she asks, trying to sound casual.

"You tell me . . . I thought I heard you talking. Like you were yelling. Are you with someone?"

"Only Raymond and Juihan."

I glare at her. Seriously? Is this the time for jokes? Doc shrugs and mutters an inaudible apology.

What is wrong with you? I mime.

Sorry, she mouths.

JC doesn't seem happy to leave it at that. We hear him lift the first set of tarps. As his steps come closer, I try as best I can to hide behind the stretchers the Stark-Lius are on.

Our self-proclaimed leader is now just a few yards from us. I hold my breath and hope he doesn't see the purple of my spacesuit through the translucent tarp.

"Are you sure everything's okay?" JC asks, sounding suspicious.

"I'm sure! I'm just struggling with all this. But don't worry. Everything is fine." She even adds an unnecessary smile to try to make herself seem more believable. I think she's panicking as much as I am.

"You need help?" he asks, his hand reaching between the tarps.

"JC! You can't come in here!" Doc's yell surprises us both.

JC stops dead, his arm still in the air. "Why?" His tone sounds more and more suspicious.

"It's a sterile area!" Doc says.

"Oh."

"If you want to come in here, you have to disinfect your spacesuit. And then you have to be careful where you step. There's blood and guts everywhere in here."

The argument finally seems to convince him. The best lies are seasoned with truth.

"Um, okay, if you're sure you don't need help . . . I'll leave you then. I still have a lot of tasks to do. . . ."

"Okay, see you later!" Doc says.

JC takes a few steps back. As he is about to leave the lab, he stops and asks, "Hey, now that I think about it, have you seen V this morning? Apparently, no one has seen him since yesterday. That's *strange,* isn't it?"

I think I can see a few drops of sweat beading on Doc's forehead.

"V?" she finally answers. "No, I don't think so. But as you may have noticed, I'm pretty busy."

I take back what I said about lies. Sometimes, the best lies are the biggest lies.

"Okay. If you do hear from him, tell him I'm looking for him?"

"Mmm hmm," Doc says, pretending to be half-listening.

JC finally leaves the lab and then MedBay. It takes a few minutes before Doc or I move or speak. I hold my breath so long I almost choke.

"Why is he always after me?" I whisper when I'm absolutely certain JC is gone.

Doc shrugs and doesn't answer.

"Do you see why we need to use the test?" I say. "Otherwise, it will be like this until the end. No one will trust anyone, and we will live in fear . . . until we die—or turn into monsters. Is that what you want, Doc? I understand that your test isn't 100 percent reliable, and that it might not prevent a deadly outcome for everyone. But it's our only chance, so we'll have to deal with it."

Doc listens to my arguments. Still, I see it in her eyes: the hesitation is getting to her. Damn her perfectionism! She'll have to learn to let go. If she's not ready to make this decision, I'll have to make it for her. If she won't let us use her test, I'll have to blow up this ship and all of its occupants—human or not—with it.

She must feel how tense I am because she tries to de-escalate things. "Let me just explain the test to you. Then we'll try it on the two of us so you can see. Then we'll decide. Together."

I reluctantly accept her proposal. It wouldn't be nice to argue now that she's made a concession. We'll see what it's like and if it's even possible to have all the survivors take the test quickly.

Doc then launches into technical explanations. I don't understand much of her gibberish, but I wait patiently. I nod or raise an eyebrow at regular intervals. Then she finally gets to the point.

"The test itself is very simple."

Back on the other side of the lab, where there are no bodies, she pulls out some small pieces of equipment from a drawer. She grins and waves a cotton swab near my face.

"A cotton swab? That's your test?"

She laughs. "Yes! It's basically the only thing I need. Well, almost. A small saliva sample, and presto! In a few minutes, we'll know if either of us is infected or healthy."

"And it took you all this time to think about it?"

"V! You can't just pull this kind of protocol out of nowhere. . . . Not to mention that I had to do all this with a very small sample. It's almost a miracle in itself that I have achieved something that works! And . . ."

"Relax, Doc. I was kidding. I am so impressed with every-thing you have done. Now, how about we actually do this?"

She nods and gets to work. She lifts her visor, slides the cotton swab into her mouth, and rubs the inside of her cheek for a few seconds. Then, she places the entire slimy thing in a small petri dish and closes the dish lid immediately.

"What is that?" I ask.

"A small colony of mold."

"And they'll tell you if you're an impostor or not?"

"Precisely. The purpose of this alien, like that of any virus, is to spread and multiply. This one is particularly tough. It can develop on next to nothing. Like on mold. So, if my saliva is infected, there will be a reaction: the alien will try to take possession of the fungus to grow in it. If there's no reaction, it means I'm healthy."

I look in the petri dish. The initial mold seems to be doing well, because nothing is moving in there.

"Well, it seems like you've been cleared by Detective Mold!"

"Yes."

"You don't seem surprised."

"I have tested myself several times already while developing this. But it's a good thing to know that I haven't been infected in the meantime!"

"Could we be infected without knowing it?"

"I doubt it, but it's a good question."

"And what would happen if you put contaminated saliva in there?" I point at the petri dish.

"Oh, I can show you if you want!"

"What? Show me? Are you hiding an alien in here?"

"Hmm, kind of."

She goes over to a small cabinet and pulls out a glass cube. Inside, there's a small piece of flesh that is anything but human.

"You're shitting me, right? Doc?"

"What?"

"What if that thing escapes? Can you imagine?"

"Don't worry, V. That thing is almost dead. I got it from Juihan, and I've kept it alive as best I can ever since. But that's not going to be enough. I don't think it will last very long."

She looks at it like it's a pet, and I try not to gag. How can she be stupid enough to nurture an alien life-form that could kill us all in an instant?

Doc looks annoyed. She explains that, without it, she would never have been able to develop such a reliable test so quickly. Despite my reluctance, I have to admit that it was worth it.

"Okay," I say. "Show me then. What happens when the mold gets infected?"

Doc clears a space on the table and places a large metal tray on it. It looks charred. Then she takes out a petri dish and opens it. She carefully runs the swab along the half-dead alien residue. With her other hand, she motions for me to step back.

"If I were you," she says, "I would watch carefully."

At that, she throws the cotton swab into the petri dish. As I stare at the mold, I can sense Doc moving and doing something behind me. The reaction doesn't take long. The fungus moves, and bubbles form in the dish. The whole thing turns bloodred, and it smells funny.

"Okay, did you see it?" Doc asks me, panting.

I nod without looking away from the dish. The alien is getting stronger and growing before my eyes.

Suddenly, there's a big whoosh next to me. I jump and turn to Doc, who's holding a massive lit blowtorch. She burns everything: the alien, the mold, the petri dish. A few long seconds later, there's nothing left on the metal tray but a small pile of smoking ashes. And no sign of life.

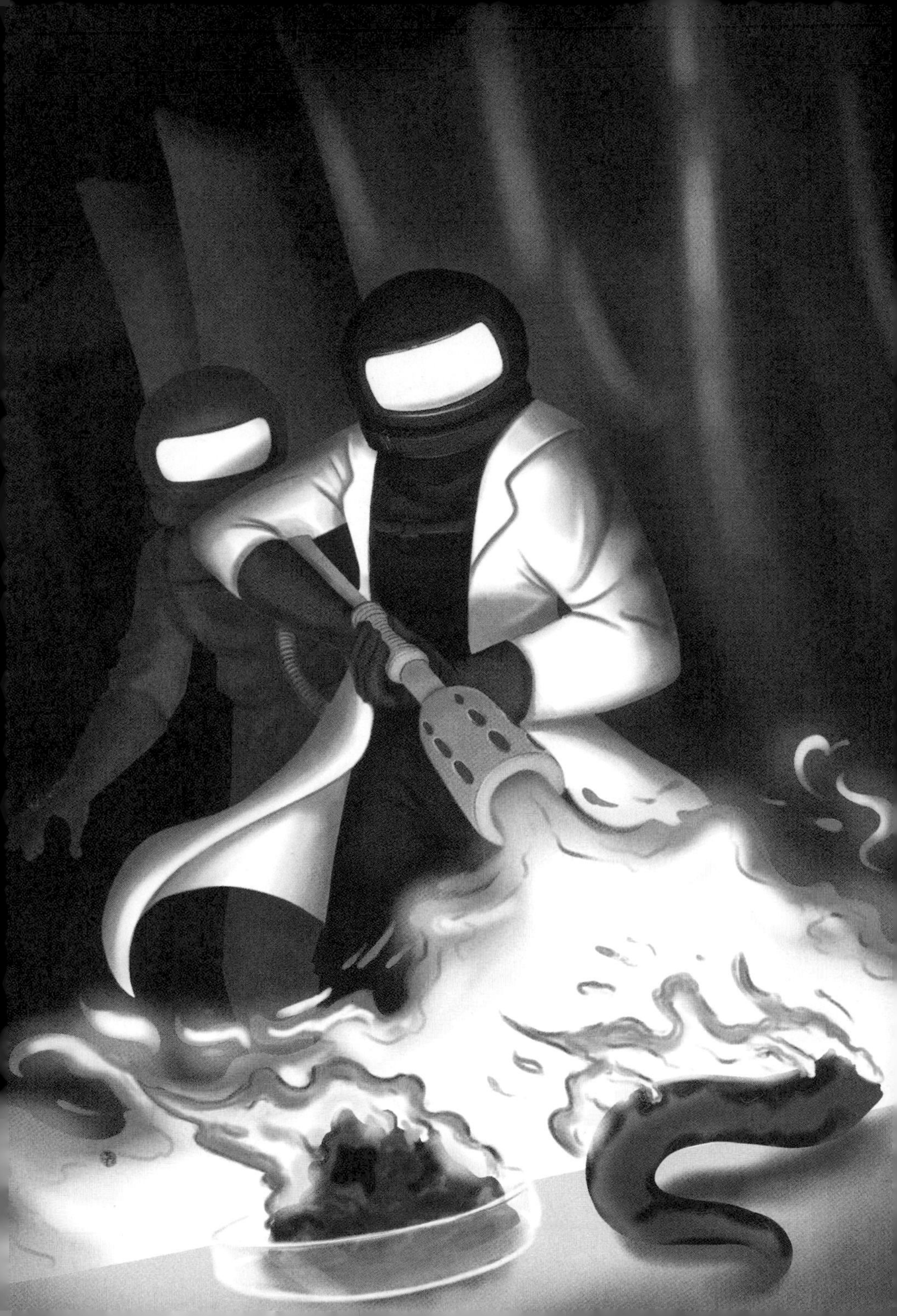

Chapter 17

For a few minutes, neither of us says a word.

Then, Doc finally breaks the silence. "Your turn, then?"

I nod in response. After putting the metal tray away, Doc places a new petri dish full of mold on the table.

As she swabs my cheek, I can't help but worry. What if I was infected without knowing it? What if my test fails within the 5 percent error margin? Would the crew choose to eject me? Or would Doc just torch me right here without a second thought? I gulp loudly just thinking about all this.

When she's finished taking my sample, Doc hands me the cotton swab. With a quick eye movement, she makes me understand that I'm going to have to put it in the petri dish myself.

"Why me?" I ask, surprised.

"Just in case," she says, grabbing the blowtorch.

For a moment, I plunge into doubt. Is this test really a good idea? What will happen if my saliva turns this mold into a bloodthirsty mini-alien? I'm not sure I'm ready for what's to come. . . . *Come on, V, buck up! Just do it: 3, 2, 1 . . . go!*

I toss the cotton swab in the petri dish and immediately step back. Beside me, Doc is staring at the dish and gripping her blowtorch, ready to light me on fire if she needs to.

With all this stress, my mind is going in circles. What if this is all a trap? What if Flavius is right and Doc isn't who she claims to be? What does she want with this ship? What if I'm falling into a trap? What if I just volunteered for a test that will bring about my own death? Why the hell did I place my trust in her so readily and blindly just because we were friends as kids? Frankly, it's a miracle that I'm still alive right now. Then again, I might not be for long.

I look back toward the petri dish. I can't look Doc in the eyes in case the test results are positive. I stare, stare, and stare at the mold mixed with my saliva. Nothing is happening. Is time standing still? Or is it slowing down? Or can I actually say that I am not infected?

"Congratulations!" Doc declares. "You are not an impostor, V!"

Doc puts the blowtorch down at her feet and gives me a broad smile. Judging by the sparkle in her eyes, I think she is also more than relieved to see that it's only me in my body.

With the pressure of all that dissipated, I can finally consider what just happened. "We don't have many suspects left now."

Doc's smile slips away in a split second.

I move closer to her. "Doc, I understand your reluctance . . . but it's just . . . time is running out. We don't really have a choice anymore."

"I don't know, V. What if . . . what if everyone's test results are negative? What do we do then? Do we just assume that

Juihan's death is circumstantial and declare everyone innocent? Will we make everyone take the test again, knowing full
well that it's not reliable and that anyone who tests positive
will argue that their first test was negative? What if . . ."

"Calm down, Doc, calm down."

She pauses. I give her a moment for her breathing to return
to normal.

"I don't think we have a choice. If there is even a small
chance that it will work, we need to take it. And if it doesn't
go as planned, we'll figure it out. We can even just go back to
the good old voting method."

Doc lets out a long sigh. I think I've convinced her. She's
going to do it.

"Fine. You're right . . ."

"Great! Thank you, Doc!"

I'm about to hug her when she stops me.

"Just . . ."

"Just what?"

"Just give me two hours."

"What for?"

"Just to check a few more things. Let me refine this if I
can. That's all I ask: two hours. After that, I promise, we test
everyone and do what we have to."

I'm not exactly thrilled with the idea. Two hours with an
impostor prowling among us . . . It's practically an eternity.
Especially since we've already been cooped up in the lab for
a long time. Who knows what's going on out there?

Maybe it's just the two of us left.

"What if something happens to you?" I ask, concerned.

"You know what to do. You know how the test works and where everything is. You won't need me."

"Doc, you can't be serious."

"Two hours, that's all I'm asking. You can camp out in front of the MedBay door to keep watch, or glue yourself to cams if that'll make you feel better."

It's my turn to let out a sigh. "Fine. You've got two hours. Try not to die, okay?"

"I'll do my best!" She starts to smile again.

I leave the lab and MedBay discreetly, clenching my teeth. Two hours is a long time. Who knows what could happen? Doc's idea of camping out here in the hallway or watching the cams isn't bad in itself, but it would draw way too much attention to me. More than I've already got coming my way. I haven't forgotten that JC is looking for me and is probably ready to try to take me down by any means necessary.

I decide to pick up my tasks where I left off before Doc pulled me into the lab. I head to Admin, where I have a few tasks left. In the hallway, I meet Alice as she's leaving Shields. She comes into Admin right after me. I position myself in front of the terminal for a likely endless upload, and she sits in front of the electrical panel to fix wiring.

"You're back at your tasks already?" I ask.

She jumps in surprise, then turns to me for a few seconds before returning to her wiring. She does all this without saying a word.

I shrug. I thought we had decided to divide her tasks. But maybe Alice would rather work than stay locked up in her pod. I get it. When I was in her situation, I did everything I could to keep busy. Anything was better than thinking about *them*. As soon as I could, I got out of the Polus district where we lived. I pushed the whole thing as far back in my brain as I could to cope.

For Alice, it must be worse. All she can do is stay in a ship filled with memories, walking the hallways where both her parents lost their lives. My heart swells with compassion. I can't leave this poor kid all alone at a time like this.

Alice finishes her task, but she doesn't leave the room. She walks over to me, then stops in front of the card reader. On my screen, the upload is still in progress. It's not even half done. I let out a long sigh, then try to start a conversation again.

"You know, Alice, I lost my parents too. I was even younger than you when it happened. It was during the war. The Great Defense."

Alice doesn't flinch, but I can tell she's listening. She's swiping her card through the reader over and over, each time with the same small error beep. I can't help but let out a quiet laugh. I struggle with that card reader too. You have to swipe it at just the right speed. That thing is so shoddy.

My download is coming to an end.

When I approach her, Alice puts her card away without completing her task. I get it. It's so frustrating that we all give up at some point and come back to it later. When she pulls out her wallet to put the card in it, I see a family photo of her and her parents, all wearing their bright outfits. My heart sinks again. I take out my card and validate her task for her.

For once, I have no trouble finding the right sliding speed for the device—not too fast or too slow; it's almost a miracle.

"Thank you," Alice whispers.

The sound of her voice makes me shiver a little. I realize I remembered it differently. It must have been some time since anyone's heard it.

"No problem. A little collaboration never hurt anyone."

She gives me a half-smile and turns to leave the room.

"You know, Alice," I say impulsively. "If you need to talk, I'm here."

"Talk about what?" she asks, stopping in the doorway.

"About everything. Well, about your parents, I mean. What happened to them."

"There's not much to say about it," she replies bitterly. "My family was brutally murdered."

"It will pass. I promise."

"I'm not sure."

"I've been there."

"It's not the same."

"How so?" I am surprised.

"My parents' deaths were unjust."

"And mine were not?"

"They were soldiers. They were at war." Her voice is trembling.

I am about to reply that my fathers were crew and not soldiers, but at the last moment, I change my mind. Alice is mourning. It's normal that she's angry. Even more so considering her age. There's no need for me to add to her grief by arguing with her.

She looks paler than ever. I want to find a way of helping her, even if it's just something little. Just then, my stomach growls and gives me an idea.

"I don't know about you, but I'm starving!"

I sigh and sit in one of the red armchairs in front of the control panels. I pivot in my seat and, with a wave of my hand, invite Alice to take a seat next to me.

"Want to share a snack?" I ask.

Alice, still in the doorway, gives me a puzzled look.

"What about the rules?" she asks.

"The rules?"

"Have you forgotten them already? Or are you just going to pretend they don't exist?"

"I remember them, don't worry. But according to my calculations, the risk isn't that great. There aren't many of us here anyway. Doc is locked in MedBay, JC is probably glued to the cams, and Flavius has almost certainly been struggling on the same task forever. I think we'll be fine for a little while."

Alice looks convinced. She comes over and drops onto one of the plush chairs.

I take an energy bar out of my pocket and use the opportunity to check the time. Doc should be calling us for the emergency meeting soon. There's very little chance Flavius or JC will arrive in the meantime. This reassures me a little. Ever since I spoke to Doc, I feel lighter. For the first time in a few days, I think I see a way out of this mission on the *Skeld*.

I hand Alice half of my snack. She gives me a big smile as she opens her visor. I find myself looking forward to being safe on Polus again.

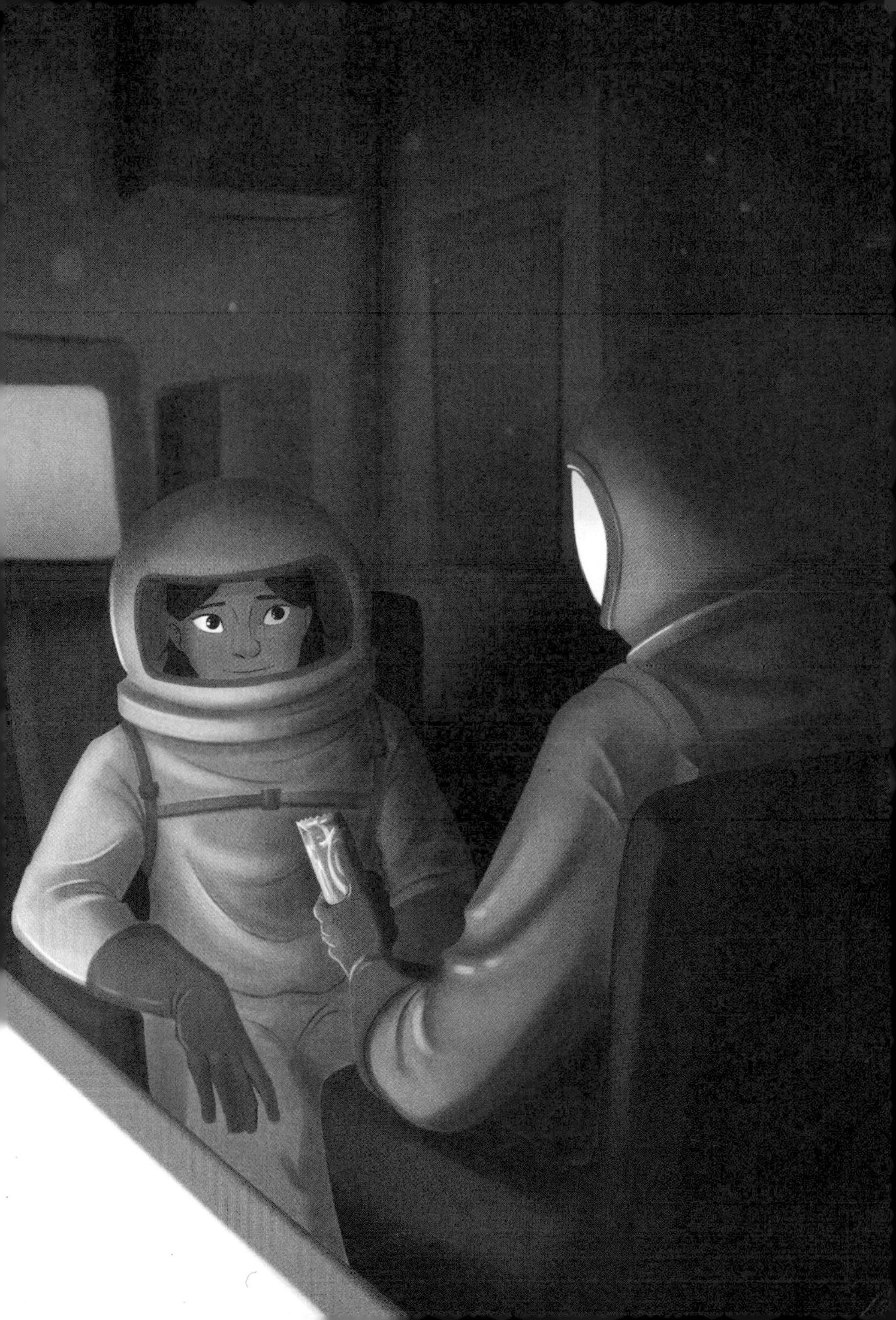

Chapter 18

I blink a few times while I try to get my head around this. In front of me, almost exactly where I left her earlier, is Doc's body. Just like Raymond's and Juihan's, her body is bisected. From the gaping wound at her middle, there are some viscous and oblong growths protruding. The infection must not have taken hold. The tentacles twitch weakly like they're near the end of their life. The process, however, seems to be far more advanced than for the Stark-Lius. I shake my head. We were this close to . . . I try not to think about it.

I turn to look at Doc's face. Her visor is cracked and covered in blood. I can still see one of her eyes. It's wide open. You can see all the terror she was feeling in her last moments. I bend down, lift her visor, and close her eyelids. If her face weren't stuck in a grimace, you might think she was sleeping.

I get up and let out a big sigh. My eyes, like my heart, are as dry as a desert. I've spent enough time here already. I have to make a decision now.

I look at the "Report" command on my visor. Would calling an emergency meeting be the best strategy? This would be my second time doing that. They'll be sure to look at me with suspicion.

Looking down at Doc one last time, I decide to summon everyone to the Cafeteria.

I'm the first one there. Flavius is next, coming from Weapons. He walks up to me but doesn't have time to say anything. JC tumbles into the Cafeteria from the south hallway, closely followed by Alice. That's all of us. It's time to get started; I don't want to make everyone wait for nothing.

"D . . . Doc is dead," I stammer. "I found her in MedBay."

My voice sounds different, slightly hoarse. I'm not sure what to expect when I break this news, but certainly not JC's reaction. Furious, he throws himself on me and grabs me by the neck.

"And what were you doing there, huh? I've been looking for you since this morning! Where have you been?"

I push him away. "Calm the hell down, JC! I was doing my tasks. Alice even spent some time with me."

"That doesn't explain what you were doing in that part of MedBay!" he yells.

"Doc wanted to talk to me," I explain.

"Why you?"

My heart rate is accelerating disproportionately. "Because she was my friend."

"Oh yeah? You're looking rather calm for someone who has just seen their friend's corpse." JC laughs.

That's when Flavius steps in. He gets between the two of us and pushes us apart. He knows what's about to happen, because he was in this situation not all that long ago. JC and I are about to come to blows.

"Woah! Let's calm down, guys," Flavius says. "JC, seriously, you can't throw that at V. Can't you tell he's not himself? This is the second friend he's lost in a really short time. How about being a bit more understanding?"

"Understanding of what, Flavius? There's a fucking impostor on this ship, and there's only four of us left. There's more to understand here. He's found two corpses. Doesn't that seem suspicious to you?"

"Sure, but I want us to try to discuss all this calmly. After yesterday's incident, we shouldn't be hasty with any decision."

"Whatever." JC pushes away from Flavius and me with an exaggerated gesture. "But I'm still waiting for an explanation, V. What were you doing over by MedBay?"

I feel my heart pounding in my chest at an unusual rate. I don't know if this is a good idea, strategically, but I decide to put all my cards on the table. We'll see if it works. "Doc was going to call us for an emergency meeting."

"What do you mean?" Flavius and JC ask simultaneously.

"This morning, she . . . she showed me something. Something that will allow us to put an end to this unbearable game of cat and mouse."

"Spit it out, V!" JC yells.

"Before her death, Doc managed to develop a test capable of detecting the virus with 95 percent effectiveness. We both took it and got negative results. She wanted to check everything before giving it to you all. . . . And if you agree to take it, we'll all know where we're at."

Strangely, JC bursts into laughter.

"What's wrong with him?" Flavius asks.

"I have no idea. . . ."

Clutching his ribs, JC looks like he won't be able to breathe soon. His laughter gradually turns into a kind of wheezing.

"Is he dying?" Flavius asks. "Hey, JC, are you okay?"

"Yes . . . yes . . ." JC manages between fits of laughter. "Sorry, V, that is just too much!"

"What?" I don't get it.

JC stands up. He seems to have completely recovered his senses. "Your test story. Did you really think we'd believe you?" He looks me right in the eye.

"But . . . why would I lie?"

"To exonerate yourself, of course. Isn't it convenient that Doc managed to develop a test that works, that she told you about it and demonstrated both your innocence and hers, and then she dies. How convenient that it's just you left to test the three of us. Did you really think we were going to do it?"

"It's the truth!" I yell. "Whoever the impostor was, they must have learned of Doc's discovery and silenced her! Unfortunately for them, she'd already explained everything to me just in case. If you think I'm an impostor, I'll take the test again, too, just to prove my innocence!"

"Don't bother. No one's going to pass your test anyway," says JC.

"And why's that?"

"Because I don't trust you. Who says this test isn't just a way for you to get rid of us?"

"But . . . I . . ." I'm panicking. "Flavius, will you take the test? You must believe me!"

The room is silent. I can read the panic and dread in Flavius's eyes.

"I don't know," he confesses. "You've got to admit that this whole thing sounds suspicious. If Doc were here, it would be different. But you . . ."

"Wait a second." I'm angry now. "Weren't you the one telling me to beware of JC last night? The one who told me how suspicious you were of him? Are you switching sides now?"

"That's not it," he says. "It's just that I'm starting to get sick of ejecting people randomly for nothing."

"Randomly! Exactly, Flavius! What I'm suggesting is a way that would allow us to make a decision based on *facts*. Not a choice based on who was most successful in defending themselves."

"I'm tired of all this." He sighs.

"But Flavius, you . . ."

JC cuts me off. "Nobody wants to take your test." He then turns to Alice. "Would you take it?"

Alice seems to hesitate, then responds, "If no one else takes it, I won't."

JC looks at me again. "You see, V? Nobody."

I stare at Alice. Is she kidding? After what we shared, I expected a little more support from her. I hide my disappointment badly, which makes JC smirk. Okay, my plan isn't going so smoothly. Fortunately, I have another one. But they don't know that. So I have to continue to play the guy defending his idea passionately.

"Do you realize what your refusal implies? Are you sure you want to be responsible for the consequences?"

Alice shrugs. Flavius looks down. A small laugh escapes JC's clenched teeth. It's not what I expected, but it doesn't change anything. Deep down, I know the outcome is inevitable now. Maybe they suspect it too somehow. That's why they're making this strange choice, a sort of desperate attempt. I can't blame them. We all do what we can with what we've got. Everyone is defending their interests.

"So, are we just going to do this the good old-fashioned way?" I ask.

"The good old method, yes," replies JC, a horrible grin on his face.

I wonder what makes him feel so confident? I don't ask. All this is far from over.

"The voting countdown ends in thirty seconds," Alice announces calmly.

She doesn't seem very concerned. No doubt she made her choice a long time ago. We'll just have to wait and see who will be voted out. Flavius seems to still be hesitating. He is shaking, panicking. He looks between me and JC, as though he could find the right answer on one of our faces. And everything will depend on his choice. But he's not the one who worries me the most. I want to know what JC has in mind. Who is he going to vote against? Does his smile hide a concern that he might be ejected from the *Skeld*? I only have a few seconds to decide. I don't want to risk having my vote not count by not deciding quickly enough.

Unsurprisingly, I choose JC. I wish I could convince Flavius to do the same, but I'm afraid that trying to influence him now would be counterproductive, and that he would end up voting against me. So I say nothing.

Have I made the right choice? I will find out soon enough.

3...2...1...

CALCULATING RESULTS.

Chapter 19

NO ONE IS EJECTED.

While this result surprises me, it's not entirely unexpected. My visor shows two votes against me, two votes against JC.

I turn to Flavius, who is staring at the ground. It looks like he wasn't ready to face the consequences of his decision. The other two survivors don't seem surprised or even concerned about this result.

JC finally breaks the silence. "Okay, let's get back to work."

Flavius doesn't need to be told twice. He slips away and down the hallway on the right, only too happy to not have to be accountable. Alice looks around the room, opens her task list, then follows Flavius out of the room. Then it's just me and JC. He's acting detached, but I swear he's watching me out of the corner of his eye.

He lets out an "Okay, let's go" and walks to the back of the Cafeteria, where he begins to fiddle with wires in the electrical panel.

I know he's just waiting for one thing: for me to leave so that he can follow me. He has no idea I can see right through him. And I swear he won't be disappointed. I intend to do what needs to be done. It's the only thing possible at this point.

Leaving JC to his fake work, I leave the Cafeteria and head to Storage. If he wants to play, then we'll play. I intentionally walk slowly.

Once in Storage, I pretend to get to work. I grab the can and pretend to fill it. To not arouse suspicion, I make it look real by spilling oil here and there. I whistle and keep an eye on the door and hallway. I bet that JC will get here any second.

And I'm right. A few minutes after I get there, JC comes into Storage. I intentionally drop my can so its contents spill on the ground. That way I've got a valid excuse to not have to leave the room right away.

"Shit," I whisper through my teeth. "Damn it. I have to start over again."

I place my can under the tank again and start the task from the beginning. While I do this, JC approaches the garbage chute. All throughout this, I stay in character as this panicked, stressed-out guy who can't complete his tasks.

I can see JC keeping an eye on me. He must not realize that I'm keeping an eye on him too. He hums an old tune while pulling down the garbage chute lever and holding it down for a few seconds. I have to be smart and responsive so that he doesn't see me watching him. And it works. I can check out the garbage can without JC seeing me watching him. And it's just as I suspected. . . .

The garbage can is already empty. JC is only here to keep an eye on me. Under my helmet, I feel a smile creep across my face, but I recover very quickly. He can't suspect that I suspect him—or that my suspicions have been confirmed.

With my not-actually-filled can in hand, I decide to go to the Lower Engine while JC continues to dump his already-empty garbage can.

Just like earlier, I go slowly enough so that JC has time to follow me at a distance. I pretend that my gas can is too heavy by holding it at arm's length and sighing and moaning loudly. I'm quite the actor! Seriously, I've got this down to an art form. It's almost sad to not have a bigger audience to witness my impressive performance.

Once I get to Lower Engine, I'll have to hurry to carry out my plan. It's all going to be a matter of timing. I can't mess up.

After I pass Electrical, I speed up until I reach the Lower Engine. When I get there, I open my can and then the tank as loudly as possible. JC needs to hear all this from the other end of the hallway. Trying to be as audible as possible, I wander through the various computer menus under my visor, hoping to quickly find the option I'm looking for. That's it. This is not a very official maneuver, and it'll require some skills, but I know I'll manage. After a few tweaks to the interface, I finally figure it out. The ship's lighting changes to a violent flashing red. On all our visors, a message appears: "REACTOR MELTDOWN INITIATED."

I stop fiddling with the engine and immediately go to the Reactor. As expected, I'm the first one there. And as expected, I hear footsteps coming up behind me.

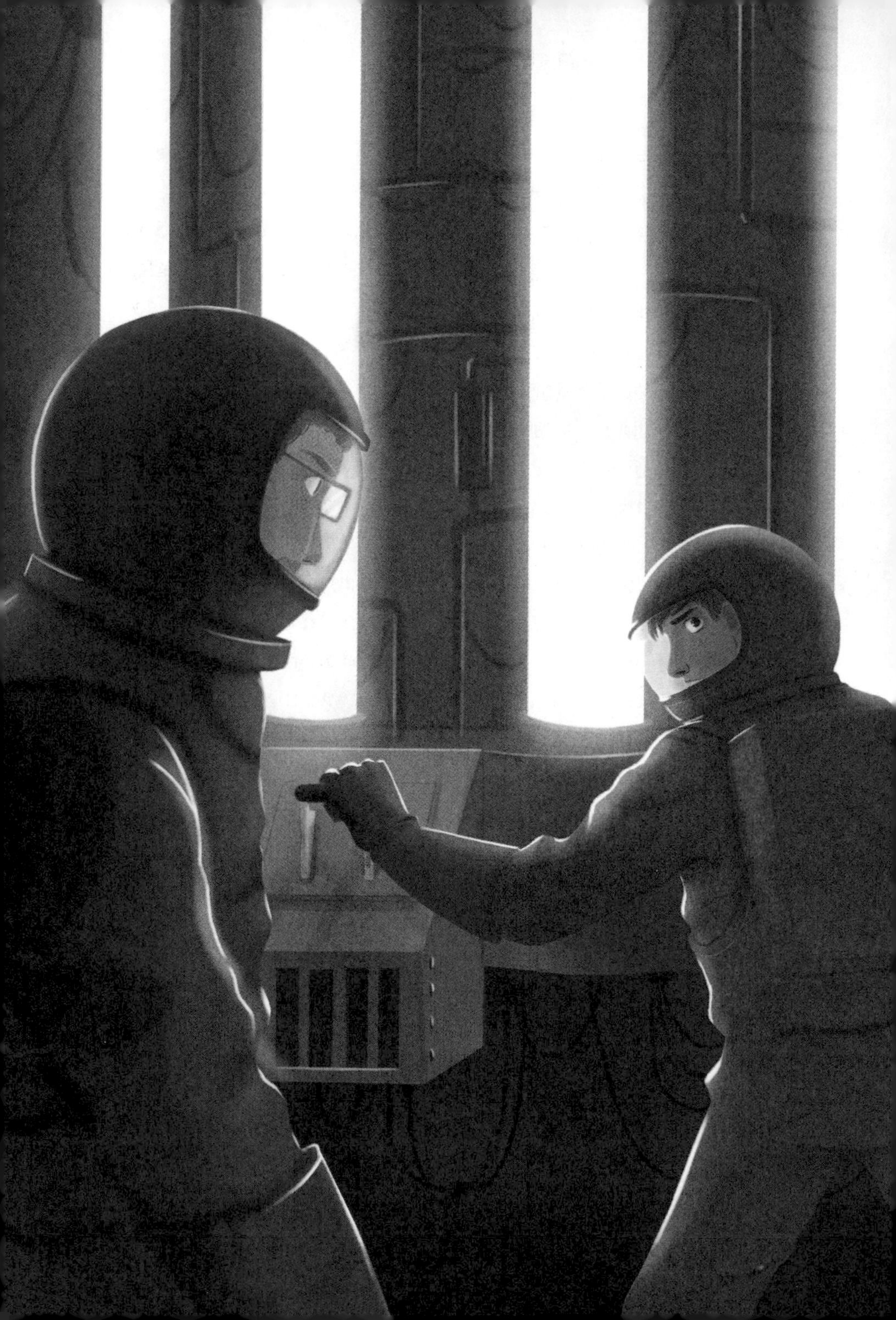

It's JC, as expected.

You won't get away with this, JC.

I wait for my crewmate a few steps from the door of the Reactor room. JC doesn't take long to get there. He's panting, and his face is all red. When he sees me in the room, he signals that I should go to the scanner on the left while he deals with the one on the right.

I nod, but I don't follow his instructions. Instead, I also go to the right and block him. He must think that I didn't understand him correctly. He tries to turn around and go to the other reader. Then I follow him there and hold him in place, my hand on his chest.

His brow furrows in disbelief. I make a fist and feel a few drops of sweat beading on my forehead. For a moment, I hesitate. But that moment doesn't last. I know that I am doing the right thing—that there's no other way. It's him or me.

JC seems to understand what is going on. He tries to back away, but it's too late. I grab him by the neck.

On the other side of his visor, his eyelids flutter, like a frightened animal facing its predator. He's looking for a way out.

JC is consumed by panic and despair. In the struggle, he hits me with a blow that I don't see coming. I don't fall, but I stumble back. JC doesn't waste any time. He rushes toward the exit. Unfortunately for him, I'm much faster. I put myself in the doorframe, blocking his way, forcing him to back away. He looks horrified, his eyes wide with fear. While trying to get away, he trips and falls.

I look down at him; he's frightened, squirming on the ground like an earthworm. He knows what I'm going to do.

As his face slowly distorts with terror and dread, he points at me. "V, what's wrong with you? I'm innocent, I swear. . . ."

I shake my head to let him know that I don't care. It doesn't matter. It's too late. I stop and listen to make sure nobody is approaching yet. I still have time, but I have to hurry.

JC creeps backward on the floor, as if he's still got a way of stopping me or escaping. But he ends up against the reactor. He's trapped. I know it. He knows it too. His gaze and his expression change from hostile to desperate. His eyes and every other part of his face plead mercy. But it's too late. I've made my decision. There's no going back.

I had warned Doc. The clock is ticking; I must hurry. I throw myself at JC. Blood spurts out all over the place, spraying the black and purple of our spacesuits. Everything is happening faster than I expected. In just a few seconds, JC's body is lifeless.

What a pity, I think.

The red light is still flashing, and the alarm is still blaring. I take a look at my visor. The cavalry should be here soon, and they'll surely be wondering why the meltdown hasn't been stopped. If nobody does anything very soon, the ship will explode in a deafening silence, without any witnesses, and without survivors. All that will remain of the *Skeld* and its crew will be some pieces of the wreck, scattered to the far reaches of the galaxy. And nobody to remember it.

As I lean over JC's body and close his eyelids, I hear foot-steps in the hallway. I quickly hide the corpse as best I can in the shadow of the Reactor, then hide myself next to it. Alice appears in the doorway. She looks around the room and doesn't seem to see me. Just as I'm about to rush toward her, Flavius comes in. For once, he's not getting here after every-thing is over. I grumble, but I know it's only a slight setback. The countdown continues. The game is not up. Everything can still go according to plan.

10, 9, 8 . . .

Chapter 20

Alice and Flavius exchange a knowing look.

7, 6, 5 . . .

She goes to my side of the reactor but passes without seeing me. Flavius is too close for me to attempt anything.

4, 3, 2 . . .

Both of them put their hands on the scanners.

The countdown stops. They've prevented the meltdown.

When the two crewmates leave the room, I let out a sigh. In the end, this is only delaying the inevitable. I've got another trick up my sleeve! Without wasting any time, I rush over to Security. There, I sit down in front of the cams. I need to know where they are.

I see Flavius first in the hallway between the Upper Engine and the Cafeteria. Alice follows just seconds later. Flavius then reappears in the hallway between the Cafeteria and Storage. Alice is following him closely. He must sense that he's being followed because he stops in the middle of the hallway. He turns around and faces Alice. It looks like he's saying something to her. I wish there were sound on these feeds! She doesn't answer and continues to advance toward him.

I bring my face closer to the monitors. I want to see every pixel of what's to come.

I don't have to wait long for things to take a gruesome turn. Alice, or at least what's left of her, is slowly changing. Large and slimy tentacles escape from her spacesuit. The sight must be making Flavius scream in horror. I can't tear my eyes away from the screen. The poor guy does what he can to try to escape, but as soon as he turns around, a sticky appendage grabs him by the waist. Then pseudopods fly out of her teal spacesuit to enter Flavius's yellow one. His body can't handle the pressure, and it splits in a bloody explosion.

Alice retracts her appendages. Captivated, I squint at the screens to see what will happen next. From each piece of Flavius, thin tentacles and other sticky membranes reach out and try to connect. Everything hinges on this moment.

Very quickly, however, these growths seem to tire. And, after one last quiver, they all stop moving.

It didn't get far this time. . . . I think.

I manage to recover quickly. Alice looks up at the camera. I have to hurry. I head for Communications at full speed! When I get there, I find that Alice arrived ahead of me. She has returned to her original form, imposing, wide, and slimy. Glorious! I smile at her, and she lets me in. I go and sit in front of the dashboard. Next to me, she sits casually in an armchair.

With one of her tentacles, she brings half an energy bar to her mouth. This gesture makes me laugh a little. If V had known what was going to happen to him, he never would have shared his snack with Alice a few hours earlier. Poor JC had

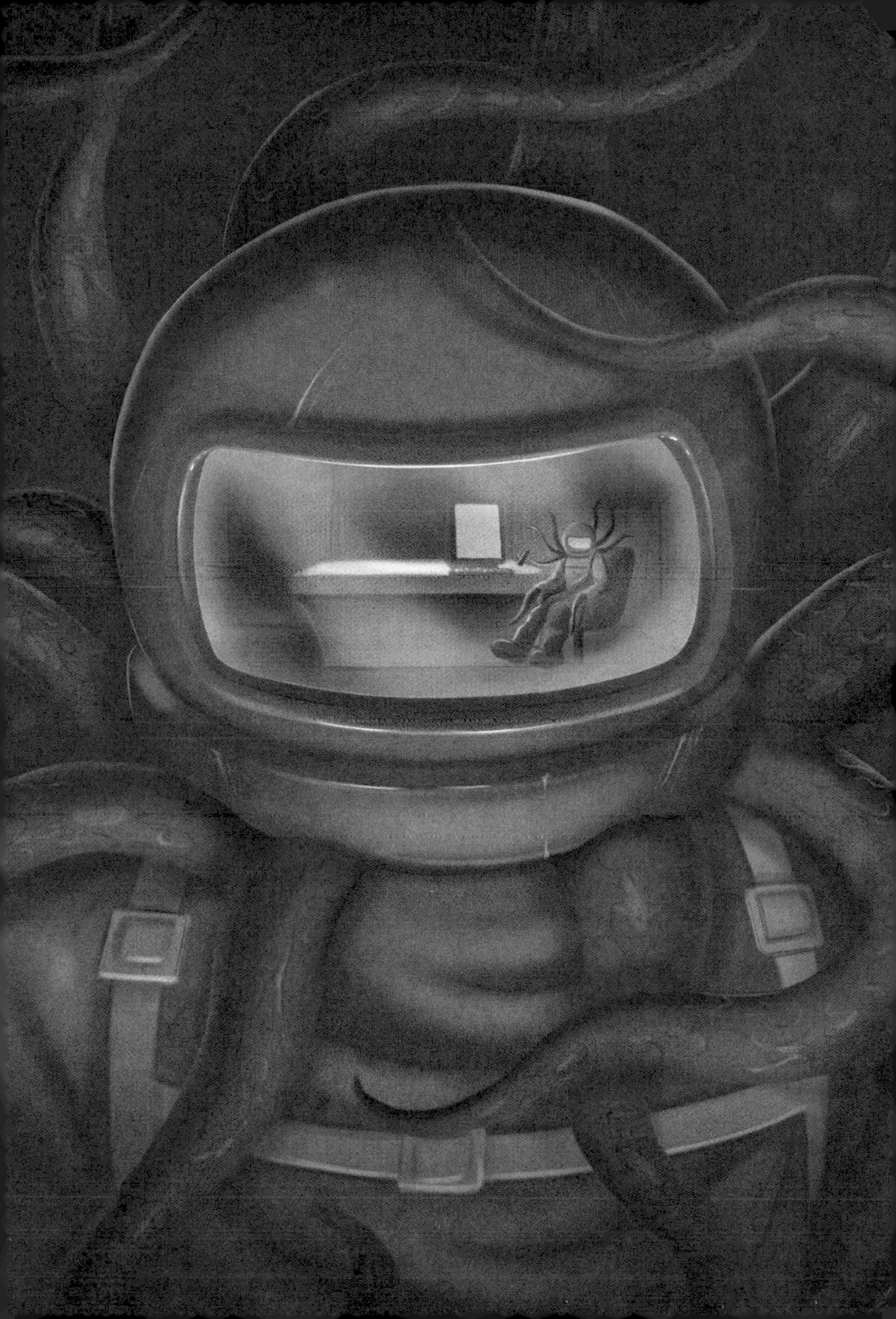

warned them not to open their visors in each other's presence! But humans, as we all know, never do as they're told.

Finally concentrating on the screen in front of me, I open all my eyes wide so I don't miss a single moment. I let out a long sigh of contentment. Using my tentacles, I type and send the following message:

MISSION ACCOMPLISHED.

SKELD INFILTRATED.

COURSE SET FOR POLUS.

WE ARE AMONG THEM.

About the Author

Laura Rivière always dreamed of becoming an adventurer, but unfortunately she lacked the courage to join the army or sail the open sea. So she decided instead to become a writer. Originally from northwestern France, Laura jumped headfirst into pop culture at a young age. She is an avid lover of sci-fi, video games, and reality TV, all of which can be found in her books along with a healthy dose of imagination.